LUCKY IN LOVE

Barbara Cartland

Barbara Cartland Ebooks Ltd

This edition © 2019

ISBNs

9781788672276   EPUB

9781788672283   PAPERBACK

Book design by M-Y Books
m-ybooks.co.uk

THE BARBARA CARTLAND ETERNAL COLLECTION

The Barbara Cartland Eternal Collection is the unique opportunity to collect all five hundred of the timeless beautiful romantic novels written by the world's most celebrated and enduring romantic author.

Named the Eternal Collection because Barbara's inspiring stories of pure love, just the same as love itself, the books will be published on the internet at the rate of four titles per month until all five hundred are available.

The Eternal Collection, classic pure romance available worldwide for all time .

THE LATE DAME BARBARA CARTLAND

Barbara Cartland, who sadly died in May 2000 at the grand age of ninety eight, remains one of the world's most famous romantic novelists. With worldwide sales of over one billion, her outstanding 723 books have been translated into thirty six different languages, to be enjoyed by readers of romance globally.

Writing her first book 'Jigsaw' at the age of 21, Barbara became an immediate bestseller. Building upon this initial success, she wrote continuously throughout her life, producing bestsellers for an astonishing 76 years. In addition to Barbara Cartland's legion of fans in the UK and across Europe, her books have always been immensely popular in the USA. In 1976 she achieved the unprecedented feat of having books at numbers 1 & 2 in the prestigious B. Dalton Bookseller bestsellers list.

Although she is often referred to as the 'Queen of Romance', Barbara Cartland also wrote several historical biographies, six autobiographies and numerous theatrical plays as well as books on life, love, health and cookery. Becoming one of Britain's most popular media personalities and dressed in her trademark pink, Barbara spoke on radio and television about social and political issues, as well as making many public appearances.

In 1991 she became a Dame of the Order of the British Empire for her contribution to literature and her work for humanitarian and charitable causes.

Known for her glamour, style, and vitality Barbara Cartland became a legend in her own lifetime. Best remembered for her wonderful romantic novels and loved by millions of readers worldwide, her books remain treasured for their heroic heroes, plucky heroines and traditional values. But above all, it was Barbara Cartland's overriding belief in the positive power of love to help, heal and improve the quality of life for everyone that made her truly unique.

AUTHOR'S NOTE

The Indian Ute tribe mentioned in this book was uprooted when the Agent in the White River Indian Company sent for military aid.

A Major T.T. Thornburgh with a troop of one hundred and eighty men was sent South from Fort Steele. They were ambushed in Mill Creek. The Major and thirteen of his men were killed.

Reprisals on the part of the Militia were forbidden by Washington and it was decided to move the Northern Utes into Utah.

Mining in the mountains flourished in the late 1880s and early 1890s and Colorado became known as the 'Silver State'.

The enormous cattle ranches lasted for only a short time. Overgrazing, the growing demand for agriculture rather than meat and a crippling cold winter in 1887 with excessively heavy snows killed great herds of stock.

CHAPTER ONE
1880

Lord Harleston looked round the ballroom of Marlborough House and yawned.

It was late and he had finished what he called his 'duty dances' and suddenly had no wish to dance with any of the beautiful women who always surrounded the Prince of Wales.

It was not only that he was not particularly interested in any one of them at this moment but also that he felt saturated with the aura of Royalty that always pervaded Marlborough House despite the fact that the parties were more amusing there than anywhere else in London.

'I must be growing old,' Lord Harleston grumbled to himself.

He knew that a few years ago he would have found such an evening absorbing and would have enjoyed every moment of it.

Now he had had enough of a good thing.

As the parties for the Prince of Wales followed hotly one after another, Lord Harleston found, whether they were given by the leading hostesses palpitatingly eager to entertain His Royal Highness or at Marlborough House where the exquisite Princess Alexandra reigned supreme, they were all very much the same.

What was more he thought that the jokes were all the same as was the extravagance, the over-rich food and bottle after bottle of superlative wines.

Because he was taking a jaundiced view of the evening, Lord Harleston was not interested, as he usually was, in the superb pictures and the treasures of the house.

He was one of the Prince of Wales's friends who really appreciated art and architecture and Marlborough House in Pall Mall, which had been built by Sir Christopher Wren for the first Duke of Marlborough, pleased him whenever he visited because it was in its own way a work of art.

It had quite a history of its own.

Originally allotted to Princess Charlotte and Prince Leopold in 1817, it had next been handed over to Queen Adelaide who lived there until her death in 1849.

Queen Victoria had asked for an Act of Parliament to be passed assigning the house for the use of the Prince of Wales on his nineteenth birthday.

Since then the Government had spent sixty thousand pounds on modernisation and additions, while one hundred thousand pounds had been spent on furniture and carriages.

In Lord Harleston's opinion the money had been well spent, although the public and the more radical Members of Parliament most definitely thought otherwise.

Now approaching forty the Prince of Wales with Marlborough House and Sandringham was comfortably housed and no one could say that he did not make the most of them.

That, however, was at the moment little comfort to Lord Harleston and yawning again he decided that he must somehow manage to go home to bed.

As he thought of it, loud laughter came from the corner of the room where the Prince of Wales was obviously enjoying himself with his friends.

The Prince's friends were another bone of contention and Queen Victoria was not alone in her disapproval of them.

The Times condemned his patronage of 'American Cattle Drovers and Prize Fighters' while other critics spoke harshly of his intimate friendships with men whose names were 'distinguished by riches rather than birth'.

Lord Harleston certainly did not come into this category, but his reputation as a rake and a roué certainly evoked the Queen's displeasure, which was, Lord Harleston thought somewhat cynically, not unjustified.

Because he was extremely good-looking, wealthy and an acclaimed sportsman, there was practically no lady in the Prince of Wales's set who would not think it a feather in her cap to captivate him if only for a short while.

A short while was indeed all it ever was, because, if Lord Harleston was bored with parties, he was equally quickly and easily bored with women.

When he pursued them, or rather they pursued him, he found that once the chase was over there were seldom any surprises or novelty in the liaison.

It was inevitable that he should therefore have gained the reputation of being a heartbreaker and the stories of his infidelity were passed from boudoir to boudoir and from beauty to beauty, as they lamented amongst themselves that even in their moment of victory they had lost him.

There was yet another burst of laughter from the Prince, echoed immediately by the remainder of the group and Lord Harleston was certain that the hilarity had been caused by the lively Portuguese Ambassador, the Marquis de Soveral.

He was noted for his wit and charm and the Prince treated him almost as if he was the Court Jester.

Lord Harleston hesitated, debating whether he should join the Prince of Wales's party or try to slip away unnoticed.

Before he could make up his mind the Prince saw him and beckoned him to his side.

"I want to talk to you, Selby."

Lord Harleston moved obediently towards the raised finger.

"I am listening, sir."

"Not here," the Prince replied in a low voice.

He slipped his arm through Lord Harleston's and drew him out of the ballroom, just as another dreamy waltz began, and along a short passage into one of the sitting rooms that had been arranged for those wishing to sit out.

Decorated with a profusion of Malmaison carnations, which scented the air, it looked very enticing with its lowered lights and cushioned sofas, but the room was empty.

To Lord Harleston's surprise the Prince of Wales closed the door behind him and walked across the room to stand with his back to the flower-filled chimneypiece.

Lord Harleston looked at him slightly apprehensively.

He was wondering what the Prince of Wales wished to say that necessitated such secrecy in the middle of a dance.

It could hardly be anything to do with finance. Although the Prince was permanently hard up, the

Sassoons and the Rothschilds were now advising His Royal Highness on his finances and Sir Anthony Rothschild, who had recently been created a Baronet, had arranged for the family Bank to advance him money when he was in difficulties.

Similar services were also offered to the Prince by Baron Maurice von Hirsch, an enormously rich Jewish Financier whose *entrée* into English Society had been sponsored by him.

The Prince cleared his throat, which gave Lord Harleston the idea that he was slightly embarrassed.

Then almost as if His Royal Highness 'took the plunge', he began,

"I really want to talk to you, Selby, about Dolly."

"Dolly?" Lord Harleston questioned him, reflecting that this was the last thing he had expected the Prince to say.

Dolly was the Countess of Derwent and Lord Harleston had enjoyed a fiery *affaire de coeur* with her. It had lasted over six months, which was longer than he maintained most of such associations before they were given the inevitable dismissal because he had lost interest.

Since both the Countess was one of the most beautiful women in England and Lord Harleston had a great many rivals, he found it amusing to have a prior claim to what many of his friends desired.

He revelled in knowing that they ground their teeth with fury every time he appeared with the Countess on his arm and she was looking at him rapturously.

That she had fallen head-over-heels in love with him had not been particularly surprising as it seemed to be inevitable in all of his love affairs.

It was, of course, in keeping with his reputation of being a heartbreaker that, when he had intimated to Dolly that everything was over between them, she had wept bitterly and thrown herself literally as well as metaphorically at his feet to beseech him not to leave her.

But even while he had tried to be sympathetic, Lord Harleston was aware that, beautiful though she was, Dolly, when one saw her too frequently, was indeed a bore.

She never said anything that he did not anticipate she would say and, if she ever made a witty remark, which was seldom, it was at the expense of one of their friends and was in a way at variance with the beauty of her face.

Somebody had once told the Countess that she looked like a Rossetti angel and she had tried to live up to that description ever since, assuming a soulful expression that had begun to irritate Lord Harleston because he knew that it was affected.

"I love you, Selby," she cried, "and I thought you loved me! How can you leave me after all we have – meant to each – other? "

It was a question that Lord Harleston had heard a hundred times before, but he had still not found an appropriate answer that did not appear brutal.

However, when he had finally extracted himself from Dolly's clinging arms, he had decided that the best thing he could do was not to see her again.

After sending her a mass of expensive flowers and a keepsake that had cost him a considerable amount of money at Cartier's, he dismissed the unpleasantness of it from his mind in a manner that had become almost a habit.

All this had happened ten days ago.

Since then a great number of notes had been delivered to Harleston House in the Countess's unmistakable handwriting, but, as he had no intention of replying to any of them, he had not even opened them.

Because it was so unusual for anyone, even the Prince of Wales himself, to talk to Lord Harleston of his intimate affairs, a liberty that he greatly disliked, he waited somewhat irritably.

"We are old friends, Selby," the Prince said in a slightly over-hearty manner, "and therefore I feel that I can be frank with you."

"But, of course, sir," Lord Harleston replied, hoping that he would be nothing of the sort.

"The truth is," the Prince went on, "that Dolly has been talking to the Princess."

Lord Harleston stiffened.

He could hardly believe that Dolly Derwent had been so indiscreet as to complain to Princess Alexandra of his behaviour.

Yet now, as he thought about it, he realised that because she had so little brain, it was in fact the sort of thing she might well do.

Princess Alexandra was deeply respected by everybody who met her. Her gaiety, her sense of fun and of the ridiculous made her play the part of wife to the unpredictable Prince of Wales to perfection.

Everybody who saw her was struck by her beauty and her extraordinarily youthful appearance, but her increasing deafness prevented her from enjoying many of the social activities that she had once delighted in.

She also, with extraordinary self-control and dignity, rarely displayed any of the jealousy she felt when her husband, although he treated her always with the greatest courtesy and respect, made it obvious to the world that he preferred the company of his 'other ladies' to that of his wife.

At the moment, as Lord Harleston knew, the Prince was deeply involved with the exquisitely beautiful Mrs. Lily Langtry and Princess Alexandra had bowed to the inevitable and raised no objection to another of the Prince's *inamoratas* being invited to Marlborough House.

There was a pause while the Prince again cleared his throat.

Then he said,

"The Princess has therefore told me to suggest to you, Selby, that Dolly would make you an excellent and certainly very acceptable wife."

If the Prince had exploded a bomb at Lord Harleston's feet, he could not have been more astonished.

He had made it a rule never to discuss his love affairs with his friends and he had also made it very clear that he had no intention of allowing anyone, and that included his relatives, to speak to him of marriage.

When he had been young, he had often been nagged by his father and mother, his aunts, uncles, cousins and anyone with the name of Harle into choosing a wife.

Young women from suitable families, almost as soon as they had stepped out of the schoolroom, were brought to his notice and the points in their favour were discussed and elaborated on as if they were horses.

He had finally succumbed simply because he was sick to death of hearing the word *marriage* drummed into his ears and proposed to the Duke of Devonshire's daughter who was both good-looking and a good rider.

He was not in the least in love with her, but, as the Duke favoured the suit because the Devonshires were hard up and Selby Harle, as he was then, thought it best to get the whole charade over and done with, he had taken the fatal step.

A month before the Wedding and with the Wedding presents arriving daily, his fiancée had run away with a penniless Officer in the Brigade of Guards whom, it was eventually disclosed, she had loved since she was a child.

Selby Harle was not by any means broken-hearted, but he did feel that he and his family had been made fools of and it was a slap in the face that he could not forgive.

He was furious, bitter and cynical not because he had lost his future wife but because he considered it was entirely the fault of his interfering relatives, who in no circumstances would he ever listen to again.

When his father died the following year and he became the Head of the Family inheriting the houses, enormous estates and a fortune that had been accumulated over the centuries, he had made it quite clear that now he was his own Master he would take advice from nobody.

In the succeeding years his relatives became rather frightened of him.

He was a law unto himself and could be ruthless if anybody incurred his displeasure with consequences extremely unpleasant for them.

In fact at this moment it flashed through his mind that he should tell the Prince of Wales to mind his own business, but he knew that it was something he could not do and, after a moment's uncomfortable silence, he said,

"I most deeply regret, sir, that the Princess should have been been worried by this trivial matter."

The Prince shuffled his feet before he continued,

"It has certainly perturbed the Princess who feels that your association with her could damage the Countess's good name. There is therefore only one reparation you can, as a gentleman, make in the circumstances."

Lord Harleston felt his anger rising inside him and for a few seconds it was impossible to speak.

At the same time he was well aware how skilfully Dolly Derwent had caught him in a trap that for the moment he could see no way of escape from.

Princess Alexandra seldom, if ever, interfered in the intrigues and love affairs taking place all around her amongst those who called themselves 'The Marlborough House Set'.

If she closed her eyes to the infidelities of her husband, she closed them as well to the way all his friends went from one love affair to another almost without drawing breath.

The majority of the ladies involved were married already and, while the lovers of the beautiful Lady de Grey, the Marchioness of Londonderry and a dozen other beauties were whispered about, gossiped over and laughed at, the

Princess remained aloof, apparently unaware of what was being either said or done.

The difference where the Countess of Derwent was concerned was quite obvious. She was a widow.

She had been married soon after she left the schoolroom to the elderly Earl of Derwent, who in his sixties still had an eye for a pretty woman and what was more significant, needed an heir.

His wife, who had died two years earlier, had presented him with five daughters and he believed, as so many men before him had, that a young girl would bring him the son he desired more than anything else in the world.

The beauty of Dolly, or rather Dorothy, as she had been christened, was further enhanced by the fact that she was healthy and came from a family of six children.

Her father was a country gentleman with no pretentions of being noble, but who was of good stock and he hoped that his beautiful daughter would marry well.

That he was overwhelmed with gratitude by the Earl's proposal went without saying and Dolly, who was allowed no say in the matter, was hustled up the aisle.

For six years both she and her elderly husband prayed that they might be blessed with a son, but finally the frustration and disappointment of it was too much for the Earl and he died.

He left Dolly an acclaimed beauty at twenty-five with enough money to live comfortably in London.

When her mourning was over, she had two or three brief love affairs with married men, who were rapturously entranced with her, but were unable to offer her marriage.

Then she had met Lord Harleston.

She had been warned about him by her friends who not only told of his reputation but assured her that she had as much chance of marrying him as flying into the sky.

"Make up your mind, Dolly," one friend had said, "that he is as unobtainable as the sun and just as hot to handle. You will get your fingers burned if you entangle yourself with him and it will spoil your standing in the marriage market."

"I can look after myself," Dolly had assured her.

They were the fatal last words of many a woman where Lord Harleston was concerned.

She had fallen completely in love with him just as experience had taught him to expect, but because Lord Harleston was quite certain that her feelings were no deeper or more intensive than her brain, he had not even listened when she had threatened to kill herself.

He had heard it far too often for it to upset him and it had become such a hackneyed phrase in his ears that he did not when he left her even give it a second thought.

She had not, of course, destroyed herself, she had been cleverer than that. She had set out to destroy *him*!

Because Princess Alexandra had made a unique position for herself in the Social world, both the Prince of Wales and Lord Harleston were aware that, when she did take a woman's part against either her husband or a lover, it was almost impossible for the gentlemen concerned not to acquiesce immediately in whatever was asked of them.

The Prince, having said what he had to say, was obviously becoming more and more embarrassed.

"I know you have made a vow never to marry, Selby," he carried on, "but you know as well as I do that sooner or later you will need an heir, a boy who will appreciate the shooting on your estate, just as I am looking forward to being invited in October."

"Yes, of course, sir," Lord Harleston murmured.

He was actually thinking that, if Dolly had not produced a son for Derwent, there was every chance, although admittedly he had been a much older man, that she might be one of those infertile women who Nature had not bestowed the blessing of motherhood on.

What was more he had no wish to marry her and was damned if he would be pressurised into it.

There was, however, for the moment one thing he could say,

"I hope, sir, you will thank Her Royal Highness for concerning herself with my life and assure her that I am deeply grateful for the honour she accords me."

He hoped as he spoke that his voice did not sound as sarcastic and angry as he felt.

The Prince of Wales, who was never very perceptive, and especially after dinner, was relieved by his attitude.

"That is *damned* sporting of you, Selby, and now let's talk about your horses. Do you intend to win the Derby?"

As he spoke, he put his arm across Lord Harleston's shoulder and moved him towards the door.

The unpleasant interview was over and the Prince could now allow himself to return to his friends with an easy conscience.

As soon as they reached the ballroom, Lord Harleston moved respectfully away and, as the Prince made no effort to detain him, he left Marlborough House.

Climbing into the small comfortable carriage he used in London he drove back to his house in Park Lane.

As soon as his sleepy valet had left him and he was alone, he made no attempt to get into bed, but stood at the window looking out over the trees in Hyde Park and wondering what the devil he could do.

He had been in many tight spots in his life, he mused, but never one like this.

He recalled how once he had slithered down a drainpipe from a second floor window when a jealous husband who suspected that he was being cuckolded had returned to his home unexpectedly when he was in an extremely compromising position with his wife.

On one occasion in France he had been involved in a duel, which fortunately had ended without scandal. Being a quicker and better shot he had deliberately merely grazed his opponent and the referee had declared that *honour was satisfied.*

There had been innumerable other occasions when he had escaped detection and exposure by a hair's breadth, but this was different, very different.

He acknowledged to himself that he had received what was in effect a Royal Command to marry a woman who he was no longer interested in and to whom he had no wish to be tied for the rest of his life.

'What can I do? What the devil *can* I do?' he asked in the darkness and the question was still ringing in his ears the following morning when he woke up.

He had left instructions with the night-footman that a message was to be sent to his friend Captain the Honourable Robert Ward first thing in the morning asking him to come to Harleston House immediately he received it.

Lord Harleston was therefore not surprised when, while he was sitting at breakfast in the morning room, Robert Ward was announced.

A good-looking attractive man of his own age, Captain Ward had served in the Life Guards until the previous year when he had retired to manage his family estates because his father, although he was taking an unconscionable time about it, was dying.

He had, however, found life in Hampshire dull and repetitive and spent a considerable amount of his time in London where he had lodgings in Half Moon Street.

He came into the morning room now looking rather white about the gills and saying as he did so,

"What has happened that you want me at this ghastly hour? I only went to bed at four o'clock!"

"Four o'clock?" Lord Harleston repeated. "I suppose you were playing cards at White's Club."

"I was on a winning streak," Robert Ward answered. "Then needless to say I lost most of it."

"I have told you it's a mug's game," Lord Harleston replied unsympathetically.

"I know," Robert Ward said sitting down at the table, "but I don't suppose you brought me here to preach to me."

Lord Harleston did not answer as the butler asked Captain Ward if he would partake of breakfast.

"For God's sake don't mention food!" was the reply. "Give me a brandy."

The butler put a glass at his side, poured some Napoleon brandy into it and then left the decanter on the table.

Lord Harleston waited until the servant had left the room.

Then he turned to his friend,

"Robert, I am in trouble!"

"Again?" his friend queried, sipping the brandy appreciatively.

"It is really serious this time."

Because of the way he spoke Captain Ward put his glass down on the table and looked at his host.

"What can you have done, Selby?" he asked. "I rather imagined that you were fancy-free at the moment."

"I was until last night."

Captain Ward raised his eyebrows.

"At Marlborough House?"

"Exactly, at Marlborough House!" Lord Harleston repeated.

Robert Ward rose and poured himself out some more brandy.

"You had better tell me about it. Thank God your brandy is good! I am beginning to feel better."

"That is more than I am," Lord Harleston countered.

"I am listening."

Robert Ward sat ready to listen carefully and, almost as if he could hardly bear to say the words, Lord Harleston told his friend exactly what had happened the night before.

He knew as he finished that Robert was listening to him with such wide-eyed attention that he had not even raised his second glass of brandy to his lips.

There was silence and then Robert exclaimed,

"Good God! I would never have thought that Dolly Derwent had the intelligence to do anything so clever as to confide in Princess Alexandra!"

"I cannot believe she had the brains even to plan it," Lord Harleston said scathingly. "It must have occurred after a tea party or something when she found herself alone with Her Royal Highness. Then, because she has been weeping and whining all over London, it all came out."

"That would not surprise me," Robert agreed. "But what are you going to do about it?"

"What can I do?"

"Marry her, I suppose."

Lord Harleston brought his fist down on the table with such force that the silver and china on it rattled.

"I am *damned* if I will settle down with her for life! She already bores me to distraction."

"It will bore you more not to be invited to Marlborough House, Selby, and the Princess can be pretty difficult if she is thwarted."

Both men were silent knowing that this was true for, although Princess Alexandra appeared so sweet, gentle and beautiful, it was recognised amongst those who knew her well that she could be very obstinate, unpredictable and at times inconsiderate.

One of her Ladies-in-Waiting had confided to Robert Ward that the Princess paid little heed to the welfare of those who served her and she herself had often received a sharp blow from her Mistress's long steel umbrella for some offence during a drive in an open carriage.

When this same Lady-in-Waiting was discovered to be having a mild flirtation, it was nothing more than one of the Gentlemen-at-Arms, she was packed ignominiously off to the country.

She was not allowed to return to London for six months, while the Gentleman-at-Arms was cold-shouldered by the Princess for almost the same period in an obvious and very uncomfortable fashion.

There was a long silence while Lord Harleston wondered frantically what he could do and felt as if he was trapped so completely that he was already handcuffed and leg-shackled in the bonds of Matrimony.

Robert sipped his brandy until his glass was empty.

Then he exclaimed loudly,

"I have an idea!"

"What is it?"

"There is only one thing you can do unless you agree to marry Dolly."

"What is that?" Lord Harleston asked dully.

"Go abroad."

"What good will that do?"

"Don't be stupid, Selby. If you are not here, you cannot marry anyone. If you can stay away for a few months, the whole thing will blow over and be forgotten. What is more there are plenty of men courting Dolly, as you well know, and it is ten to one that if you are out of reach she will find somebody else's arms preferable to no one's."

Lord Harleston sat up.

"Do you think that it is possible?"

As he asked the question, he was thinking that he had aroused passions in Dolly Derwent that she had never known before and his long experience of women had taught him that once they had tasted the fires of love it was hard for a woman to live without them.

He then thought how much it would depress him to be exiled. He would miss the Derby and not be able to watch his horses run at Royal Ascot.

Then sharply, as if he had made up his mind, he asserted,

"Anything would be preferable to being married!"

"Very well, that settles it," Robert said. "You go abroad."

"But where? Where shall I go? Paris is too obvious. Besides, the Prince will take it as an insult if I choose to visit a City where he always enjoys himself so tremendously rather than obey his command."

"No, of course, you cannot go to Paris!" Robert agreed at once as if his friend was being particularly stupid. "Let me think."

He put his hand to his forehead and groaned.

"I feel as if my head is packed with cotton wool."

"Have another brandy."

"I will in a moment. I am thinking."

Again there was silence.

Then suddenly Robert made a sound that was almost a cry.

"I have it! I know exactly where you can go, Selby."

"Where?" Lord Harleston asked without much enthusiasm.

"To Colorado!"

"Colorado?"

The way he spoke sounded as if Lord Harleston had not even heard of the place.

Then, before Robert could reply, he enquired,

"Are you suggesting that I should try digging for gold?"

"No, of course not. You have enough of that already," Robert answered. "But have you forgotten that only a month or so ago you told me that you had put quite a considerable amount of money into the Prairie Cattle Company?"

Lord Harleston started.

"So I did!"

"I was rather amused at the time," Robert went on, "thinking it a new investment I had not heard about before. That fellow at White's, I cannot remember his name, persuaded you to go into it, saying it is being backed by British capital and has more than fifty thousand head of stock and controls more than two million acres in Colorado's Plainlands."

"Yes, of course, I remember now!" Lord Harleston exclaimed. "Like you I thought it sounded interesting and a change from railways and shipping."

"Well, there you are. It never does any harm to have a look at where you have put your money."

"Are you seriously suggesting that I should go to Colorado?"

"You know the alternative without my repeating it."

Lord Harleston did not speak for a moment.

Then he gave a short laugh that had no humour in it.

"Very well, '*Needs must when the Devil drives*!' I will visit Colorado."

CHAPTER TWO

As *The Etruria* ploughed through the heavy seas, Lord Harleston could only be thankful of Cunard's boast that in forty-three years they had never lost the life of a passenger and in the previous thirty-four years never a letter.

No other company could say that and it gave Lord Harleston a feeling of safety even though *The Etruria* seemed very small and the Atlantic very large.

The Etruria was actually one of the biggest ships to cross the Atlantic and, although there was always talk of building bigger ones, Cunard still held the Blue Riband.

The ship was, from the tourists' point of view, the greatest luxury afloat.

With her two funnels and three masts she was large enough to provide for those who could afford separate State Cabins rather than communal ones and they were heated by steam and lit by gas.

Lord Harleston, resentful at having to leave England when he had no wish to do so, was however thankful that his secretary, the excellent Mr. Watson, had at the very last moment managed to obtain for him not only one State Cabin but two, the second being hurriedly converted into a sitting room.

This meant, he knew, that he would not have to associate with his fellow travellers and one glance at them was enough to tell him that he had no wish to do so.

Only because Lord Harleston expected efficiency, and Mr. Watson was a past master in that respect, was it possible for him to leave London immediately after luncheon and to go aboard *The Etruria* in Liverpool just before she sailed at midnight.

The sea voyage would take at least ten days, which Lord Harleston contemplated grimly, but Robert had tried to console him when he had bid him 'goodbye',

"Whatever discomforts you have to suffer, Selby, remember it will be all over in four or five months' time while marriage is expected to last a lifetime."

Lord Harleston had shuddered and he was already wondering what the Prince of Wales would think when he learned that his victim had flown.

He had, however, contrived with Robert's help to make his departure seem a coincidence and certainly not a contrived effort to evade the Royal Command.

Accordingly Lord Harleston had written to the Countess of Derwent what he hoped was a clever letter.

She had given him the opportunity because, while they were still talking in the breakfast room, the butler had tendered to his Lordship a note from her on a silver salver.

With one glance at the pale lilac-coloured paper and the writing that was already scrawled over several dozens of notes in the drawer of his desk, Lord Harleston was about to wave it away when the look on his friend's face made him pick it up.

Immediately the butler left the room Robert suggested,

"I should open it."

"Why?" Lord Harleston asked bluntly.

"It might be a good idea to know if she has already been informed that the Prince of Wales has spoken to you."

"Yes, of course, Robert."

Lord Harleston opened the letter, read it and said,

"It contains nothing more sensational than an invitation to dinner this evening."

He did not add, because it was none of Robert's business, that there were also many fulsome expressions of undying love that he had heard before.

"Good!" Robert exclaimed. "That gives us just the opportunity we need."

"What do you mean?"

"You must tell her that you are leaving England. It would be a mistake just to disappear."

Lord Harleston considered this for a moment and then agreed.

"Very well, Robert, come into the study and tell me what I should say."

When the letter was completed, they both considered it somewhat of a masterpiece.

Lord Harleston had written,

"*My dear Dolly,*

It is with the deepest regret that I cannot accept your charming invitation to dine with you this evening, but unfortunately I have just learned that a relative of mine who is in America is in dire distress.

This means that I must do my best to be of assistance and am accordingly leaving for New York today.

I am sorry I could not call so that you could wish me 'bon voyage' and I am bitterly disappointed that I now have to cancel my parties both for the Derby and Royal Ascot.

With all best wishes,

Selby."

"Excellent!" Robert applauded. "I like the rather subtle way that you have avoided saying whether the relative in question is male or female."

"I know what Dolly will suspect," Lord Harleston replied, "but she will not be able to prove it."

He then rang the bell and, when almost at once Mr. Watson came into the study, the wheels of the 'Harleston Machine', as Robert called it, were set in motion.

For the next few hours his valet, assisted by several footmen, packed his clothes, Mr. Watson brought him a dozen letters and papers that required his signature and Lord Harleston gave his friend precise instructions about what he wanted him to do while he was absent.

"My box at the Derby is, of course, at your disposal, Robert," he said, "and the same applies to the one I use at Royal Ascot. Make it clear that you are not acting as a Deputy in my absence, but entertaining on your own account."

"Some people will be surprised that I can afford it," Robert commented with a twist of his lips.

"Make it appear to everybody, especially the Prince of Wales, that I was very upset at having to go away at a moment's notice. You must, however, be extremely vague, again especially to the Prince, as to when I am likely to return."

"And when will that be? "

"When you write and tell me that Dolly's affections are engaged elsewhere," Lord Harleston answered, "and the Prince of Wales has forgotten that I disobeyed his instructions."

"I think he will miss you."

"I hope he does," Lord Harleston replied. "It means that he will look forward to having me back and I can assure you, Robert, that I shall be only too eager to return home."

"You may enjoy yourself in America," Robert hazarded.

"I have never had any wish to see America," Lord Harleston replied. "Although some Americans we have met are good company and the women very attractive, I have always felt that Europe was more likely to be my spiritual home than the Wild West."

"You never know," Robert answered, "and don't forget when you reach New York to call on the Vanderbilts. When they were over here last year, they pressed you, rather over-effusively I thought, to stay with them, but your answer was very evasive."

"I will certainly call on them," Lord Harleston replied, "but I am not certain that I wish to be the guest of anybody until I have looked around."

Robert smiled.

He knew that Lord Harleston was not only fastidious in the choice of his intimate friends but also he took great care not to be too friendly with those he had no affinity with.

At the same time he personally liked William Henry Vanderbilt, the son of Cornelius, who had died three years ago.

It was William Henry Vanderbilt whose remark, '*the public be damned!*' had been quoted and requoted, who was now President of the New York Central Railroad and the richest man in the world.

Robert had enjoyed being in his company on his last visit to England, although he had said somewhat cynically,

"The trouble with rich men is that their golden aura seldom rubs off on those they associate with."

"I think you will find," Robert went on now, "that you will know quite a lot of people when you do arrive in New York, but don't forget that you have decided to go to Colorado. I want to hear your opinion of it and I only wish I was coming with you."

"If I cannot stand being alone," Lord Harleston replied rather haughtily, "then I will send for you."

"There is nothing I would like better," Robert answered, "but you know I cannot leave my father. The doctors say he might die at any moment."

"I am sorry," Lord Harleston nodded sympathetically.

"Actually it would be the best thing that could happen. Half the time he has no idea about what is happening and the other half he is in pain."

"I only hope that never happens to me," Lord Harleston exclaimed. "I would prefer to die cleanly and quickly from a bullet!"

"I feel the same," Robert agreed.

Because everything was organised for him so efficiently, Lord Harleston had only to change into his travelling clothes and step into the carriage that was waiting outside the front door for him.

Mr. Watson accompanied him to the Station and handed him over, as if he was a very precious parcel, to the Stationmaster resplendent in top hat and gold braid.

A compartment had been engaged for him on the Express that was to carry him up to Liverpool at what was considered an astronomical speed.

When he had said 'goodbye' to his secretary, Lord Harleston settled down to make himself as comfortable as possible.

Every published newspaper and every magazine of any interest was provided for him in his compartment and there was also a hamper of food in the preparation of which his chef had excelled himself as well as several bottles of wine.

Had there been time Lord Harleston would ordinarily have had his own private coach attached to the train.

But as it was, he had to make do with a reserved carriage to himself with the comforting thought that his valet and his luggage were in another one adjoining it.

Because he was tired, having stayed awake most of the night before worrying, Lord Harleston spent part of the journey sleeping.

He arrived in Liverpool to find the Stationmaster waiting for him with two carriages to convey him to the docks where he would board *The Etruria*.

There he was welcomed aboard as if he was Royalty.

The Cunard Company had instilled into all their employees the importance of making the public feel that they were welcome, especially those who were titled.

They were also determined to make the passage across the Atlantic very different from the days of the first Cunarders, which were profoundly uncomfortable.

When their ships had been no more than the size of seaside resort Steamers, the paddlewheels and machinery took up all the space amidships so that the passengers' quarters were fore and aft where they felt the worst of the movement of the sea.

Lord Harleston found himself remembering Charles Dickens's description of the tiny cabin that he and his wife had occupied during their first American tour.

When Dickens entered, he found two berths one above the other, the upper being an almost inaccessible shelf which he derided,

'Nothing smaller for sleeping in was ever made than a coffin.'

One thing certainly not to be found on *The Etruria* was what had been on Dickens's ship, a special deckhouse with padded sides to shelter the ship's cow whose milk was reserved for women, children and invalids.

Lord Harleston's valet, Portman, who was well used to travelling with him, soon had everything 'shipshape' as he appropriately called it.

His Lordship's trunks were unpacked with those 'not wanted on voyage' stowed away below and in the sitting cabin there appeared as if by magic two decanters containing his Lordship's sherry and brandy and in an ice bucket a bottle of his favourite champagne.

There were also books provided by Mr. Watson that Lord Harleston was amused to note included a popular *Guide to America.*

Finally there was even a vase of Malmaison carnations, which unfortunately reminded him of Dolly, from his own greenhouses in the country.

"Will you be dinin' below, my Lord?" Portman asked.

Lord Harleston considered for a moment.

"I think I will have dinner in my own sitting room this evening, Portman," he said, "and tomorrow I will take a look at the Dining Saloon."

Although he had never been to America before, Lord Harleston had travelled frequently on the P. & O. ships that sailed to the East and knew that the first night at sea was always something of a scramble.

It was traditional that ladies did not wear evening dress on the first night at sea and it was, Lord Harleston knew, a mistake to be in a hurry to choose a place at one of the tables in the Saloon that afterwards he might regret.

He expected by right that he would be placed at the Captain's table, but, if he thought that did not suit him, he could always demand a table for himself.

Anyway it was clearly better to wait and see what turned up.

The food that he was provided with in his cabin was good and the service supervised by Portman was excellent.

Yet, as soon as he was alone and his valet had retired for the night, Lord Harleston began to feel lonely and, as he had told himself with a twist of his lips, homesick for England.

Although he had been bored last night at Marlborough House, the picture that remained in his mind was of the beautiful women dancing beneath the crystal chandeliers and the men laughing at some witty saying by the Marquis de Soveral.

It now seemed infinitely preferable to setting off on what was an unwelcome adventure simply because he had been forced into it.

It was all Dolly's fault and he thought that he would never forgive her for making so much trouble with Princess Alexandra.

"Damn all women!" he swore aloud. "I shall become a misogynist."

He knew as he spoke that this was *very* unlikely.

At the same time he hoped that it would be a very long time before he would become interested, let alone infatuated, with another woman however alluring or attractive she might be.

He forced himself to think about his horses.

Then, almost as if his conscience was being arraigned in the dock, he found himself thinking back over the women who had been a part of his life in the last five years.

There was an uncomfortably large number of them and he found it extraordinary that none of them had made any deep imprint even on his memory.

They had, of course, all been beautiful and amusing and at times he had found them irresistibly desirable and had risked both their reputations and his own to make love to them.

But now he kept remembering the cynical Frenchman who had said, '*in the dark all cats are grey*' and thinking it over he had to admit that it was indeed true.

'I shall never marry,' he decided yet again.

Then he knew that this was a decision that he would have to change.

Of course some time he had to marry. It was absolutely essential that he should have a son to carry on not only his title, which was comparatively unimportant to him, but the long tradition of Harles who had lived in the great mansion in Buckinghamshire since the time of King Charles II.

Many of them had served their country in a manner that ensured the family name was repeated again and again in every history book.

'Damn it, I am proud of my blood!' Lord Harleston reflected almost defiantly.

But it meant that sooner or later he must succumb, as other men had before him, and marry if only to have sons and grandsons before his life ended.

Anyway there was plenty of time, he decided finally and, as he was both disgruntled and tired, he moved into his other cabin and climbed to bed.

Surprisingly he slept well and awoke to find that they had run into a turbulent sea.

This meant, Lord Harleston thought with some satisfaction, that most of the passengers would stay below, which would leave the deck comparatively empty when he took his exercise.

He had always proved himself to be a good sailor, despite having encountered tempests in the Bay of Biscay, mistrals in the Mediterranean and once a very unpleasant typhoon in the South China Sea.

But whatever the weather, Lord Harleston was determined to have his exercise, which was something he never missed wherever he might be.

In London, as in the country, he rode every morning. He hunted strenuously in the winter and played an extremely good game of polo at Hurlingham Club during the summer.

Besides this he employed professionals he could play tennis and racquets with and, having found during his years in the Army that he was quite a good pugilist, he often had a bout or two with the Army champions at Waterloo Barracks.

After breakfast, which Portman had brought him early, he went walking round the deck despite the fact that the waves were breaking threateningly over the bow.

As he had expected, there were very few other passengers brave enough to face such unpleasant conditions.

After an hour's exercise Lord Harleston went back to his cabin to read some of the books that Mr. Watson had provided him with.

They fortunately held his attention and, when he went down to the Saloon for luncheon, he looked round hopefully, thinking that it would be pleasant if he could find one congenial soul who he could strike up an acquaintance with.

He was, however, disappointed.

A large number of the men looked to him like commercial travellers or businessmen and there were two or three excessively plain women and no one he had any wish to have a conversation with.

Lord Harleston was not the sort of man who liked drinking with strangers in the smoking room and he was far too astute to think of playing cards or any other game of chance on board a ship.

As if the solicitous Cunard Company had realised that the only thing they could not guarantee to provide for the enjoyment of the passengers was congenial company, they made up for it by providing what was often described as 'ten meals a day' for their First Class passengers.

The day began with grapes and melons. Then breakfast the first meal was described as being 'able to provide anything on earth'. At eleven o'clock there was a cup of *bouillon* and at noon sandwiches were carried round the decks.

During the rest of the day, interspersed between luncheon, tea and dinner, there were trays of ices, coffee and sweets and the gastronomic marathon ended at nine o'clock with supper.

As Lord Harleston was a small eater, because he liked to keep his weight down for racing his own racehorses, the idea of eating 'right through his ticket' did not appeal to him.

As there was little else on board to look forward to, he was heartily glad when the ship reached New York and he had his first sight of the Statue of Liberty, which was under construction.

Despite his rather casual response to Robert's suggestion that he should call on the Vanderbilts, he had instructed Mr. Watson to send them a cable announcing his arrival.

He was therefore not surprised when he was greeted immediately the ship docked by one of Mr. Vanderbilt's secretaries informing him that a carriage was waiting to carry him to their house on West Fifty Second Street.

Lord Harleston accepted the invitation gratefully, largely because he was by now considerably tired of his own company.

Travelling in the extremely comfortable carriage that had been opened so that he could appreciate his first view of the City, Lord Harleston learned from the secretary who accompanied him what had been happening in a place that had grown phenomenally quickly in the last few years.

He was obviously anxious to impress on Lord Harleston how civilised the Americans had become.

He informed him that Henry Irving and Ellen Terry had just made their New York debut and that the first New York Telephone Exchange had issued its first telephone directory with three hundred names.

"We have also grown very keen on photography, my Lord," he continued, "and the stars of the new Metropolitan Opera House on Broadway are all having their photographs taken."

Lord Harleston attempted to look impressed.

Then to his surprise, as if he was a greenhorn from the country, the secretary began to warn him against the 'tricks and tracks' in the great Metropolis that it was important for strangers, especially foreigners, to be aware of.

Lord Harleston, who was a very experienced traveller in other parts of the world, was amused as he listened to tales of gamblers who regularly worked the trains and how at a hotel a visitor should guard against being robbed by the owners of skeleton keys.

Watches were snatched in the street and railroads abounded with pickpockets, many of them women.

The secretary ended by advising his Lordship not to buy a belt advertised for five dollars that was guaranteed to make the wearer invisible!

Lord Harleston laughed.

"You are quite safe there. It is something I have no wish to be!"

"You have no idea, my Lord, of the crookedness and vice that is growing up in this City as well as the buildings," the secretary informed him solemnly.

"I am very grateful to you for warning me," Lord Harleton replied and was relieved when they reached the Vanderbilts' residence.

It was after the death of his father, the Commodore, that William Henry Vanderbilt decided to build himself a Royal mansion.

His builders had urged him to use marble, the loftiest expression of power, but Mr. Vanderbilt was afraid of marble, thinking that in its cool shine there lurked an evil eye.

He had good reason for such a conviction because both William Backhouse Astor and another millionaire had died soon after their mansions of marble were completed.

Mr. Vanderbilt had therefore ordered instead three massive brownstone houses, one for himself and two for his daughters, employing several hundred American workers and fifty foreign craftsmen.

"The house is not yet complete," the secretary informed Lord Harleston, "but I don't think your Lordship will be uncomfortable and I am sure that you will enjoy Mr. Vanderbilt's collection of paintings, which have been acclaimed as sensational by all who have viewed them."

The whole house, Lord Harleston thought when he saw it, was not only sensational but had almost a nightmare quality about it.

The overwhelming doorways like triumphal arches, the gilded ceilings curved like sections of Egyptian mummy cases and the clutter of vases, lamps, figurines and rare books, made him feel that he must be seeing double after drinking too much the night before.

There was no doubt of the warm welcome he received from Mr. Vanderbilt and, as his bedroom was the size of a ballroom, he could hardly complain of being cramped.

And it was Mr. Vanderbilt's daughter-in-law, Mrs. William Kessain Vanderbilt, who welcomed Lord Harleston more effusively even than her father-in-law.

She had always been socially ambitious and the mere fact that she had a distinguished and rich English Nobleman in her hands made her start buzzing around him like an excited Queen Bee.

Lord Harleston was soon aware that unless he was careful he would find himself married not to Dolly but to some unfledged American girl, who was allowed no thoughts of her own being manipulated by her mother like a puppet on a string.

Mrs. William Kessain Vanderbilt, who had been Alva Smith of Mobile, produced young women like rabbits out of a hat for Lord Harleston's approval.

It was difficult to explain that he had never at any time in his life been interested in girls, that he had no idea what to say to them and no intention, if he could help it, of dancing with one.

But, as night after night there was a dinner party given in his honour, followed by a dance afterwards, Lord Harleston quickly decided that he would move on.

What spurred his decision to take flight even more quickly was his learning that Alva Vanderbilt was planning a Fancy Dress Ball.

If there was one thing Lord Harleston really disliked and he was determined not to take any part in, it was a Fancy Dress Ball.

He always avoided them in England despite the fact that the Prince of Wales had almost gone on his knees to beg him to attend one that rivalled the extravagance of the splendid fêtes presided over by the Prince Regent at Carlton House eighty years earlier.

Sir Frederic Leighton, President of the Royal Academy, had been called in to supervise the decorations at Marlborough House where over one thousand four hundred guests had been invited to appear in fancy dress.

The Prince, who was sensationally garbed as King Charles I with a black felt, white plumed hat blazing with diamonds, opened the ball with a Venetian quadrille.

The music played on until dawn, supper was served in two enormous tapestry-hung scarlet marquees and even Mr. Benjamin Disraeli, who arrived late and not in fancy dress, having been at the Mansion House, described the whole affair as 'gorgeous, brilliant, fantastic!'

The only dissenter, in fact the only person who received an invitation but deliberately absented himself, was Lord Harleston.

"I am damned if I will make a fool of myself to please the Prince of Wales or anybody else for that matter," he had told Robert. "Could anything be more ridiculous than a lot of grown men dressed up like ninnies, prancing about with wigs on their heads!"

"Where is your sense of fun?" Robert had asked him mockingly.

"Fun? Do you call that *fun*?" Lord Harleston snorted. "I would rather roll about on the grass on Hampstead Heath with a pretty girl."

Robert laughed.

"Who would not?"

Now to Lord Harleston's dismay Alva Vanderbilt had said,

"I visualise you as Sir Galahad or perhaps you would prefer to be Hamlet, Prince of Denmark. You would look so handsome, Selby, in either costume."

Lord Harleston made it quite clear that unfortunately he could not play either role.

"It's very sad, Mrs. Vanderbilt, after you have been so kind," he stated, "but I have an urgent appointment to meet a friend in Denver and will have to leave tomorrow morning."

Mrs. Vanderbilt gave a shrill shriek of protest and despair.

"But you cannot. It's impossible!" she declared. "I have arranged this ball especially for you!"

"It's more disappointing than I can possibly say," he replied, "but unfortunately my delightful visit to your father-in-law has to come to an end."

Alva Vanderbilt was a determined, intelligent, unhappily married woman, who had no other outlet except her social ambitions.

She always had her way with her family because she wore them down, but with Lord Harleston she had met her match.

He left just as great pots of flowers in huge vanloads were being carried into the ballroom to provide a background for the ponderous and costly supper that was to be served by impeccably trained servants in maroon livery.

Thinking of the profusion of Dresden shepherdesses and shepherds, Portias and Venetian Princesses, *pierrots* and highwaymen who would be capering round the ballroom to the strains of a hundred violins, Lord Harleston settled down in his drawing room in the sleeping car for the long journey to Denver with a sigh of relief.

"I have had a lucky escape, Portman," he told his valet as the train moved out of the Station.

"You have indeed, my Lord," Portman replied. "I can't see your Lordship enjoyin' yourself dressed up and, if you asks me, them things are a dreadful waste of money!"

"That is something that never appears to trouble people in this country," Lord Harleston remarked drily.

He felt that the Americans still had a long way to go to learn how to make the best use of their enormous and ever-increasing wealth.

As Denver was more than halfway across America, he took a long time to reach it and by then he was becoming curious about the country itself and the gold rushes that had altered the whole character of what had originally been wild cattle country and before then Indian territory.

The first excitement of gold mining had attracted men eager for the precious ore from all parts of the world to try to cash in.

Between 1859 and 1870 over twenty-seven million dollars' worth of gold was extracted from streams and mountains in Colorado.

But the first miners had skimmed off only the surface and later had been obliged to sink deep shafts.

However the gold that was supposed to solve everybody's problems was not as easy to find as had been supposed and the State became beset with poverty.

The Indians had chosen this time to stage a revolt against the white man's intrusion into their lands and, although a good number of peace moves were attempted by the whites, the situation grew increasingly worse.

In the literature that he could find on the situation, Lord Harleston learned that by 1864 Indian attacks on the freighting roads grew increasingly frequent and ranchers and farmers were murdered and scalped in surprise raids.

But by now things had begun to settle down because the railways had been developed and, while this was being hailed jubilantly, silver and lead were discovered and once again Colorado began to expand.

It did this very quickly and the population trebled and quadrupled while the railroads created new towns and encouraged the establishment of agricultural settlers.

Because Lord Harleston liked to be knowledgeable about anything that he was involved in, he read everything he had with him about the financial situation in Colorado and found himself extremely interested, although he had not expected to be, in the development of mining apart from his own personal investment in cattle.

'While I am here I might as well see everything,' he mused.

He learned, which he had not known before, that the discovery of rich carbonates of lead and silver ores in the mountains close to Leadville had led to an enormous rush of miners and speculators to the district two years ago and which was still continuing full blast.

He was not certain what he expected to find in Denver, because his reading had now given him an entirely different idea of what the place might be like from what he had previously expected.

But at least, he ruminated, it might be more amusing than he had anticipated and he began to make a list of the stories he would relate to Robert when he returned home.

He also thought it was a pity that he and Robert could not have been exploring together as they had done many times in the past.

Then there had always been situations that amused them both, which would keep them laughing, and even the dullest party or the longest of journeys would seem less arduous and certainly less dreary because they were together.

'Perhaps his father will die and he will be able to come out to me after the funeral,' Lord Harleston thought optimistically.

Then he realised that, after hours of driving over flat barren country with little sign of human habitation, he was nearing the City of Denver.

As it was cloudy, there was no sign of the Rocky Mountains, which he knew could not be far away since Denver was a mining centre.

That it was spoken of as a place that was unusual and definitely interesting made Lord Harleston glad that his long journey was coming to an end.

At Denver he had arranged to meet a man who would show him the cattle that he had invested his money in as a great number of other British people had done.

The Prairie Cattle Company was entirely British financed and he had already learned that British Companies were now speculating in the Colorado mines.

'I shall think twice before I do it too,' Lord Harleston decided.

He had read so much about the seams that had petered out and the men who had been tricked out of their claims or murdered because they had been successful, that he was not prepared to gamble on something that had to be taken on trust and which could not be proved until the digging had finished.

Now, as if even that prospect began to pale on him, he thought,

'I don't intend to stay here long and I must begin to think about where I shall go next. God knows the country is big enough for me to have a wide choice.'

Even as he thought of it, he suddenly felt depressed because his thoughts kept returning to what was happening in England.

Tomorrow, although he had forgotten it until this moment, the Derby would be run at Epsom and, if his horse did win, which he confidently expected, he would not be there to lead him into the Winners Enclosure.

"*Blast and curse all women!*" he exclaimed out loud as the train puffed slowly and purposefully, black smoke belching out of its funnel, into Denver Station.

CHAPTER THREE

As Lord Harleston stepped out of the train, he was relieved to find a tall good-looking young man waiting for him with outstretched hands.

"You must be Lord Harleston," he began. "I'm Waldo Sheridan Altman Junior. Just call me 'Waldo'. I've come to welcome you on behalf of my father."

"How do you do."

"I hope you've had a good journey," Waldo went on. "My father was notified by your Lordship's secretary that you were coming to Denver and we've also received a telegram from Mr. William Henry Vanderbilt instructing us to look after you."

He was obviously considerably impressed by this recommendation and his voice held quite a reverent note in it as he spoke of the great man and this amused Lord Harleston.

They proceeded outside the Station to find two open carriages and, without waiting for Portman, who was being assisted with the luggage by one of Mr. Altman's men, Lord Harleston set off with Waldo Altman at his side.

He guessed that the young man was about twenty-four years of age and was obviously very conscious that he had been put in charge of a celebrity in his father's absence.

He was also anxious to impress him with Denver and what had been achieved in the City.

Lord Harleston thought that Denver was extraordinary considering where it was situated.

He had not expected a massive Gothic style copied from the Cathedrals of Europe or the flat roofs, loggias and cupolas of Italy.

He had learned already that it was the largest City in the State of Colorado not only from a mining point of view but also as a principal stage and freighting post.

As they drove on and he could see that Denver's architecture owed its inspiration to Romanesque, Greek, Moorish and Oriental styles, he could only think that it was certainly unique and undoubtedly often fantastic.

While he was looking, Waldo was talking.

"My father wants to invite you to come out to his Ranch as soon as you've seen enough of Denver."

"I should much enjoy it," Lord Harleston replied. "I am only sorry that nowadays one cannot see the buffalo that were there in such profusion in the past."

"I agree," Waldo nodded. "There are a few of them left, but the great herds were slaughtered and exterminated in the most outrageous fashion. Now you'll see so many cattle you'll never want to eat meat again!"

He laughed as he spoke and, because he was young and seemed full of the joys of life, Lord Harleston laughed too.

"First, my Lord, you have to see Denver," Waldo continued. "And I think we'll have some surprises for you."

Lord Harleston wondered what they would be, when at that very moment as the carriage turned into what was obviously the City's main street, he saw coming towards him a four-in-hand driven by a woman.

Besides her and on top of the coach there were six other very attractive young women dressed elegantly but flamboyantly, two of them holding small lace-trimmed sunshades over their heads.

It was such a surprising sight that Lord Harleston stared in silence and, as the four-in-hand drew nearer, he saw that the woman driving was exceptionally attractive and so were the other passengers.

"Who is that?" he asked.

Waldo chuckled.

"I thought they'd surprise you."

"They do indeed and the woman driving is obviously extremely experienced with the reins."

He thought as he spoke that he could not remember when he had last seen a woman driving a four-in-hand.

The woman he was looking at had large dark eyes, a mass of black hair, besides crimson lips and mascaraed eyelashes.

As the two carriages passed each other, he was aware that the women on top of it were obviously either actresses or belonged to a still older profession.

They were laughing and, as they waved to Waldo, who obviously knew them and waved back, they made a very pretty picture, which was certainly something that Lord Harleston had not expected to find in Denver.

"See you this evening, Waldo!" one of the women called out.

"That's a date, Bessie!"

Then the vehicles had passed each other and Lord Harleston looked at his companion for an explanation.

"I don't know whether you have heard of 'The Row' in Denver?" Waldo asked as they drove on.

"*The Row?*" Lord Harleston questioned.

"I guess that's a Westerner's description of it," Waldo said. "You'd call it 'the Red Light district'."

"That is what I guessed," Lord Harleston admitted, "but I have not heard it called 'The Row' before."

"We also speak of it as 'The Line'," Waldo informed him. "It's the street where the parlour houses, cribs, variety halls, saloons and gambling dens are congregated."

"They certainly advertise themselves very cleverly," Lord Harleston commented drily.

"It was Jenny Rogers's idea to drive her 'goods' around the town and as you've guessed she's an expert with a horse whether she is driving or riding it."

"I thought that."

"She only came here last year and before that she was known as the most beautiful 'madam' in St. Louis."

Lord Harleston's eyes twinkled.

"Then I presume Denver thinks it is lucky to have her."

"You bet we do," Waldo agreed. "She's given The Row class and, when I take you to her house in Market Street, I'll wager you'll not find better in Paris or any other City in Europe."

Lord Harleston was about to say that he had no wish to visit a brothel, knowing very well that they usually bored him.

Then he thought that not only would he sound pompous but he might as well see what Denver's entertainments were, although he had certainly not expected anyone as attractive as Jenny Rogers.

Because he thought he would be interested, Waldo began to explain the arrangements in Denver for the men who flocked there from the mountains or came in from the Prairies.

As it was all so different from what Lord Harleston knew occurred either in London or Paris, he listened intently to Waldo.

"Because we're a new town," Waldo was saying, "the parlour houses and the cribs are generally side by side in the same block, but you'll find, my Lord, the crib layout in the Colorado mountains is usually a frame building where a door and one window leads onto the street."

He paused and, as Lord Harleston did not say anything, he added,

"They are cheap and ghastly, but you will see the crib girls at night dressed in low-cut, short-skirted dancehall gowns leaning out of the windows and luring in the customers!"

"There are, I imagine, a large number in every mining town," Lord Harleston remarked.

"Of course," Waldo answered, "but the Denver parlour houses provide us with our real entertainment."

Lord Harleston raised his eyebrows wondering what this would be and Waldo explained,

"The best houses have two or three drawing rooms, each with a piano, and also a ballroom for dancing. What's more some have banquet rooms and the food's better than you'll get at the hotels."

Lord Harleston looked surprised and Waldo went on,

"There're two really smart houses in this town. One belongs to Mattie Silks, who was the reigning Queen of

'The Row' before Jenny came along and now she's having her nose put out of joint."

Waldo would obviously have said more if at that moment they had not arrived at a surprisingly large and impressive building, which, he explained, is his father's house.

Lord Harleston saw that it boasted features from a French Château combined with a Cathedral spire and chimneys like triumphal arches.

"I hope we'll be able to make you comfortable, my Lord."

"I am sure you will," Lord Harleston replied, "and I shall look forward to meeting your father."

Then he asked Waldo,

"You have not told me if your mother will be here."

"No, she'll be at the ranch with Pa and as we'll be here on our own we can enjoy ourselves."

He looked at Lord Harleston quickly as he spoke to see if he thought that this sounded too familiar and then reassured he carried on,

"Pa and Ma won't approve of my showing you the gaieties of Denver like Jenny Rogers, but I can't believe your Lordship wants to spend hours talking to the Councillors and hearing how they're improving the sewers!"

"God forbid!" Lord Harleston exclaimed and they both laughed.

The inside of the Altmans' mansion was as fantastic as the exterior with a profusion of pot plants, velvet hangings festooned with fringes, statues and pictures that made Lord

Harleston shudder, although the Oriental carpets and much of the furniture were surprisingly good.

He realised that Denver's citizens were attempting to build up a new Society in a place that only a short while ago had been an open desert.

Since they had first started they had endured a disastrous fire, which had burned down the original houses and the camps set up by the first settlers, and this was followed the next year by a devastating flood.

It was amazing that so much had been achieved and from his reading Lord Harleston had learned that new arrivals were pouring into Colorado at the rate of over five thousand a week.

"I know you have new silver mines at Leadville," he remarked.

"We certainly have," Waldo replied, "and millionaires are being created overnight."

Lord Harleston looked interested.

"Tabor, a general storekeeper whom I know quite well," Waldo went on, "grub-staked two prospectors for about sixty-four dollars. They found the Little Pittsburgh mine when silver ore fetched two hundred dollars a ton. The storekeeper began investing in other mines and is now Colorado's Silver King. After being Mayor of Leadville, he is now Lieutenant Governor of the State."

"That is certainly quick work!" Lord Harleston laughed. "Have you been gambling in the same way?"

"I promised my father to keep my money in cattle," Waldo replied. "Equally I shouldn't be tempted to keep all my eggs in one basket."

"I am sure that is wise."

It struck Lord Harleston that the same applied to him and, while he was here, he might try to make some money in the mines as well as with cattle.

The more Waldo talked about silver and gold the more interested he became.

It was obvious that all the mountains in this part of the State were worth prospecting, but he recognised how quickly a seam could run out and that, unless one was particularly lucky, it was far easier to lose money than to make it.

'I shall certainly be cautious,' Lord Harleston reflected to himself.

By the time Portman had arrived from the Station with his luggage he was ready to go to his bedroom to have a bath and change for dinner.

"I could have given a dinner party for you tonight," Waldo said, "but, if I'm to take you round the town, I thought that any guests I invited would talk their heads off and we'd never get away."

"That was thoughtful of you," Lord Harleston replied, "and personally I would prefer that we should be alone."

He realised with amusement that he had no choice but to allow Waldo to show him the town.

He guessed that it was the height of entertainment for the young men to visit the parlour houses and, as Waldo was offering Denver's best, it would have been churlish to ask for anything different.

The bedroom that Lord Harleston had been allotted was large and the huge ornamental brass bedstead looked likely to be very comfortable.

There was a profusion of carpets, curtains, chairs, *objets d'art* and plants that reminded him of the overcrowded mansion of the Vanderbilts and made him realise that the rich are always inclined to acquire too much and to suspect that simplicity proclaimed poverty.

"Well, at least we don't have to put up with a minin' camp, my Lord," Portman said with a grin.

"That is certainly a blessing," Lord Harleston agreed, "and I daresay we shall be quite comfortable until we move on."

He was giving Portman a warning as he spoke not to settle in for he was well aware that, like most English servants, he preferred to stay where he was rather than explore new places.

By the time Lord Harleston had bathed in what seemed very modern and sophisticated surroundings, such as he had also found at the Vanderbilt house, and had changed into his evening clothes, he was in a mellower mood.

While he was dressing, every sort of drink was offered him from whisky to champagne, but, as he preferred to be abstemious, he had only drunk a small glass of sherry before he went downstairs to find his host.

Waldo was waiting for him and, when Lord Harleston appeared, he looked at him before he exclaimed,

"Now I know what's wrong with my clothes!"

Lord Harleston realised at once that in England Waldo would certainly have appeared outlandish, while he was quite certain that his appearance was *de rigueur* for a young man about Denver.

"Where can I get togged up like that?" Waldo asked him.

"By coming to London."

"I have heard that's what the swells in New York are doing, but I didn't believe it!" Waldo replied. "Now I understand why they're ambitious to look English, even though they resent you."

"Why should they do so?" Lord Harleston asked.

Waldo hesitated before he told the truth.

"Because we think you're always looking down your long noses at us!"

Lord Harleston chuckled.

"I assure you it's not true, but perhaps we may give that impression because we are more reserved in our natures than you are."

"You bet you are," Waldo said, "although there are some exceptions. I met a regular guy, who might be one of your relations, recently when I was in Leadville. His name was 'Harle'."

"Harle?" Lord Harleston repeated. "What was his first name?"

"They call him 'Handsome Harry'!"

Lord Harleston frowned.

He knew quite well who Waldo was referring to and was not particularly pleased to hear that he was in this part of the world.

Every family has its black sheep and Harold Harle, who had been known as 'Harry' ever since he was a child, was a relation whom the older members of the family tried their best to forget.

His father had been a cousin of Lord Harleston's father and Harry had been the youngest of three sons.

The oldest brother had gone into the family Regiment as was customary, the second had become a sailor and Harry had been destined for the Church.

It was, however, quite obvious while he was at school and later at Oxford University that his inclinations were very indifferent to anything but the pursuit of enjoyment.

When he had left Oxford, or rather had been sent down in his last year for rowdy behaviour, he had appeared in London and was accepted because he carried the family name.

He had so much charm and was so excessively good-looking that hostesses forgave his somewhat outrageous behaviour and merely removed their daughters very quickly from his vicinity because he had no money and no prospects.

Using his charm as other men used their talents and their brains, Harry Harle became involved in one escapade after another, most of which included a pretty woman who was the wife of somebody else.

He also mounted up an astronomical number of debts which were settled by his long-suffering father and his older brothers simply because they could not allow the family name to be dragged through the Courts.

When eventually things were almost at breaking point and there was even a family conference as to whether they should allow Harry to go bankrupt, to everybody's relief he left England.

That he took with him a very attractive young woman, who was within a fortnight of her Wedding to another man, was not so relevant as that he had actually disappeared.

Later it was learned that Harry had gone to America and had married the girl who had accompanied him.

Her father, who was furious at her behaviour, cut her off without a penny although he was a rich man and refused to have her name mentioned in his house ever again.

But the Harle family gave a collective sigh of relief and hoped that it would be a long time before Harry reappeared.

Thinking of him now, Lord Harleston remembered how over the years there had been occasional news of him filtering back from friends who came from New York, Chicago or further afield like Florida and other parts of the North American Continent.

Lord Harleston remembered that once or twice there had been frantic requests for money, which Harry's father had sent, because he was still fond of his youngest son and he could not bear to think of any child of his being imprisoned for debt or on the verge of starvation.

Then, as far as Lord Harleston knew, there had been silence for some years. In fact thinking back he realised that it must be at least five or even more years since he had heard Handsome Harry's name mentioned.

"What is this man Harle doing?" he asked Waldo somewhat stiffly.

"Gambling," Waldo replied. "If he's a relation of yours, my Lord, I can tell you one thing, he has the quickest hand and is the smartest dealer of cards in the whole State!"

Lord Harleston's lips tightened.

It did not surprise him in the slightest that Harry had become a card sharper.

He only hoped that he would not be involved in any scandal while he was in Colorado.

Deftly he changed the subject and over dinner they talked once again of cattle, gold, silver and coal mining, which had only recently started in a big way.

The food was plain, the beef superb and the wine imported from France at enormous expense was drinkable.

Waldo Altman drank bourbon, but it was a spirit that Lord Harleston had no liking for and he had already decided that, if it was all he was to be offered on this trip, he would manage without alcohol.

The brandy offered him at the end of the meal was French and he accepted a glass before he asked Waldo,

"Have you had any trouble with the Indians lately?"

"I was hoping you wouldn't ask that question."

"Why not?"

Waldo looked uncomfortable for a moment,

"I don't want to frighten you."

Lord Harleston smiled.

"You will not do so."

"Well, my father and some of the local authorities are worried about the Utes."

"Who are they?" Lord Harleston asked.

"They are a tribe in the North," Waldo explained, "and their hunting grounds are on the other side of the Rockies."

"What is happening there?"

"It's not really their fault, at least my father doesn't think so, but after fifteen years of peace with the white man, the younger Chiefs are being upset by an Agent from the White River Agency."

"What is he doing?" Lord Harleston enquired, thinking that this was not particularly interesting.

"He's been obsessed with the idea of attracting the Utes away from hunting to farming. He has antagonised them, especially by ploughing up the track where they race their ponies."

"That sounds a stupid thing to do,"

"My father's afraid that, if the soldiers intervene, there will be another war. We've had quite enough of that sort of disruption in the State already and especially we want no trouble on the Plains."

"No, of course not," Lord Harleston agreed.

He had thought that all the fighting with the Indians was over, although in some of the books that he had read there were descriptions of settlers being killed, their farms burnt and the Indians scalping those they murdered.

However, when dinner was over, he realised that Waldo had no desire to go on talking and was becoming anxious to show him the town.

A comfortable carriage drawn by two horses was waiting for them outside and, as they climbed into it, Waldo said,

"The first place I'm taking you to is *The Palace*!"

Lord Harleston raised his eyebrows and Waldo laughed.

"Not your sort of Palace, my Lord, but the best our King Ed Chase can provide."

He went on to explain that *The Palace* was the first of the really elegant gambling mansions and Ed Chase was Denver's most spectacular gambling operator.

King Ed, he told him, had already opened a smart gambling games Club, called *The Progressive* with fifteen hundred dollars he had won at poker while working as a railroad brakeman.

"It owns Denver's first billiard table," Waldo boasted proudly, "hauled across the Plains by ox cart."

When Lord Harleston laughed, he said,

"Ed also introduced a three-headed freak at another gaming Club and gave the first great ball in honour of the *Nymphs du pave.*"

In case Lord Harleston did not understand, he translated,

"'The frail sisterhood' some folks call them. One person who doesn't like them is the second Mrs. Chase. She tried to shoot Nellie Belmont and then divorced Ed because he kept her in a cosy little love nest."

With such an introduction Lord Harleston looked at Ed Chase with interest when they met him at *The Palace.*

Prematurely grey with steely blue eyes that missed nothing, he usually sat at the *Progressive Club* on a high stool with a sawn-off shotgun across his knees.

The Palace was as fantastic as its owner. It had room for two hundred players and a bar decorated with a sixty-foot mirror. It was not only a gambling hall and a saloon but a theatre as well.

When Lord Harleston and Waldo arrived, there was an extremely bawdy comedienne on the stage and the programme had a verse on it that started,

"*Palace of Real Pleasure and Voluptuous Art*
Where lovely women fascinate the heart — "

Waldo pointed it out and said,

"The Dean of St. John's Cathedral calls this 'a death-trap for young men, a foul den of vice and corruption'."

After watching the female entertainment, Lord Harleston decided that the Dean might have a point.

The Palace girls were certainly enticingly alluring and, as Waldo explained, preferred gold dust and nuggets to flowers!

He also described in detail how a friend of his, having won sixty thousand dollars in a lottery, had showered jewels and furs on one of the dancers.

However, when he found out that she was married, he shot her from his box while she was performing on the stage!

"If you ask me, you are too trigger-happy in Denver," Lord Harleston remarked.

"In this country it's often a case of kill or be killed," Waldo replied.

After watching the gamblers for a short time, Lord Harleston backed his lucky number on the roulette table, let it run three times and then picked up his winnings and suggested to Waldo that they go somewhere else.

"Do you mean to say you're not going on?" he asked. "You're on a winning streak!"

"I never push my luck," Lord Harleston replied, thinking that he had not had much luck lately.

Outside *The Palace,* Waldo said that they would begin by visiting Mattie Silks, keeping Jennie Rogers as the final *pièce de résistance.*

When Lord Harleston saw the Red Light District, he certainly thought it was sensational and it was larger and different from anything he had seen before.

As Waldo had described, the crib girls were leaning out of the windows looking for trade, their customers being some very rough and dirty miners who were already drunk and a number of over-exuberant cowboys.

Mattie Silks herself was certainly a surprise.

Having previously operated parlour houses in the wild cattle-shipping towns of Kansas, she had arrived in Denver ten years earlier after a successful tent tour of the mining towns. She brought with her several lovely boarders and a tent big enough for business.

She, however, soon owned a classy two-storey brick house in Market Street with long windows shaded with awnings.

Richly gowned even for a Society lady, she was small, plump and rather pretty.

She had naturally curling light brown hair with gold streaks in it and, as Waldo greeted her with a kiss on both her rouged cheeks, she laughed and teased him before he introduced Lord Harleston.

Because she was obviously extremely impressed with a Lord, she took him into an elaborate over-decorated parlour where 'the girls', as she called them, sat about on stools while the customers lounged comfortably on sofas.

There was dancing in another room and music, which was surprisingly well played, but Waldo insisted that they were not to stay long.

After he had paid what appeared to be a large sum for some very dubious champagne, which neither he nor Lord Harleston drank, they moved on to Jennie's house, which was only a little way down the street.

By this time, having heard so much about Jennie Rogers and having seen her driving the four-in-hand, Lord Harleston was feeling quite curious.

At least, he thought, he would rather talk in Denver to an experienced madam than to a strait-laced worthy, who was certain to bore him even more than Mrs. Alva Vanderbilt had done.

As soon as they arrived at Jennie's house at 2009 Market Street, he could see that it was extremely well run. She employed a large staff of servants and a piano player who would not have been out of place on any London stage.

There were also additional musicians who played violins and other musical instruments all with an expertise which showed that they had been chosen with care and good taste.

But what was more musical than anything else was Jennie's laughter.

Six foot tall she had a wild exuberance in her eyes and it was echoed in her laughter, which seemed to ring out with a note of defiance as if she dared anybody to criticise her.

Everything in the house was opulent, plush and new since it had only been opened in January.

The girls too, who Lord Harleston realised had come from St. Louis with Jennie, were exquisitely dressed in ballgowns and behaved in a way that would not at the moment of his arrival have shocked Marlborough House.

Their job was to amuse and they were obviously past masters at it, especially their madam.

Lord Harleston found himself relaxing for the first time since he had left England and laughing unreservedly at some of the outrageous things that Jenny said and the quickness of her wit.

He had not met many American women and he had no idea they could be so sharp that they could turn the serious or dull with a turn of phrase into something uproariously funny.

As they talked, other customers arrived and Lord Harleston was interested to note that they behaved with good manners that he doubted he would find in the 'houses of pleasure' off St. James's Street.

It amused him that Jennie was making a place for herself in Denver almost as if she was a Society hostess rather than a madam of a bawdy house.

As the evening progressed, Waldo went off to dance with a very attractive girl with red hair and Jennie, looking around the room, which since the dancing had started was somewhat depleted, said to Lord Harleston,

"Is there anyone I can interest you in? Zaza is an expert in the joys of the Orient and Renée is French."

He shook his head.

"On this occasion, you will understand, I am an onlooker. I have only just arrived after a long journey and I intend to go to bed early. And alone."

She laughed.

"Good resolutions are only there to be broken!"

"There I agree with you, but not tonight."

She smiled at him without any rancour and he proposed,

"But you must allow me to buy champagne for your girls, if you permit them to drink it."

"I can't prevent them from doing so."

Lord Harleston put quite a large amount of dollars down on the table and it vanished as if by magic.

Then Jennie set out to amuse him by telling him of her struggles in St. Louis, of the way she had started to get her own business going there and to decide to come to Denver because it was the largest and richest City in the State.

She told him of her difficulties with her 'boarders' who were well paid, well fed and whose bedrooms were fashionably furnished.

Some, however, were moody and frequently so depressed that they took laudanum, which was liquid opium. It could be bought at any drugstore, but in large quantities it was the route to suicide and lethargy.

They also talked about horses and Lord Harleston found it surprisingly agreeable until, when Waldo returned after his dance, he realised that he was very tired.

"I am going back to bed," he said, "I have never been able to sleep well on a train and tonight I hope to make up for the hours I stayed awake."

"But you can't leave so early," Waldo objected.

"There is no need for you to accompany me," Lord Harleston smiled. "I have enjoyed my evening enormously, but for you the night is still young."

"That's true," Waldo agreed, "as long as you don't mind."

"I assure you, I am quite happy to go back alone," Lord Harleston replied.

"I hope you will come again tomorrow evening," Jennie suggested in an inviting tone.

"I will certainly consider it," he promised.

With Jennie at his side and Waldo just behind him, he walked towards the front door.

As they reached it, it was opened by one of the servants and waiting to come in were three men wearing dusty riding boots, wide-brimmed hats and with pistol holsters around their waists. They were obviously cowboys.

The cowboy in front held nothing in his hands, but the two behind him were carrying a woman in their arms.

"Evenin', Miss Jennie," the man in front began. "We've brought you a present."

"A present, Brooker?" Jennie echoed. "What is it?"

"The prettiest little filly you ever set eyes on."

"I don't want no more girls," Jennie replied, "and certainly none of *your* choosing."

"Hold your horses until you hear how we got her," Brooker replied. "We picked her up about six miles outside of town. The Injuns had killed her Pa and Ma and her's bin walkin' for a night and day afore we found her."

"I'm sorry for her," Jenny said sharply, "but Indians are your business not mine. Take her someplace else."

"We thought," Brooker said, "of handin' her over to them strait-laced old crows who talk about doin' somethin' for orphans, but that means they'd make her a servant. Her's too pretty for that and, if you don't take her in, she'll end up in a crib."

"I am not interested!" Jennie insisted.

"Take a look at her afore you decide," Brooker responded pleadingly. "Her's pretty as an angel and as sweet as one too."

"That's true," one of the other men said who was holding the girl, "and talks like a lady, her do. There's no one we can take her to with a kind heart except for you, Miss Jennie."

As he spoke, he pulled the blanket that the girl was wrapped in from her face and Lord Harleston saw that they had not exaggerated when they had claimed that she was very pretty.

She was obviously asleep or unconscious and her eyelashes were dark against the very white almost translucent skin of her small pointed face.

She had almost perfect features and hair that was so fair that it was lighter than the sun at dawn.

"She's certainly pretty," Jennie admitted grudgingly. "Do you know who she is?"

"She says when we first picks her up that her name were Nelda – Nelda Harle," Brooker answered.

At the sound of the word 'Harle', which he had mispronounced, Lord Harleston started.

"What did you say?" he asked.

"Nelda Harle," Brooker repeated. "Sounds strange, but that's what her says, wasn't it, boys?"

"Yeah, that's what she says," the two other men agreed. "Come on, Jennie, take her, we can't stand here a-holdin' her all night."

The men were silent while Jennie Rogers considered what she should answer.

Then Lord Harleston spoke.

"I will take her," he said. "If I am not mistaken, she is a relative of mine."

Everybody including Waldo turned to look at him in astonishment.

"But her name's 'Harle'," Jennie pointed out at length.

"My family name is Harle," Lord Harleston replied, "and if this girl is who you say she is, then I suspect she is the daughter of somebody called 'Harold Harle' who Mr. Altman was talking about earlier this evening."

"Handsome Harry!" Jennie cried. "Now we know who she is. But I never knew Harry had a daughter or a wife for that matter."

She turned back into the house saying as she did so with a jerk of her head,

"Bring her in!"

The cowboys removed their hats and, carrying the girl called 'Nelda', followed Jennie.

She opened a door off the hall and Lord Harleston saw that it was furnished as a bedroom.

There was a large comfortable brass bedstead, a great number of decorative mirrors on the walls and bright pink curtains bordered with a silver fringe.

The cowboys put the girl they carried carefully down on the bed with her head resting against the pillows.

As they did so, the blanket that she was enveloped in fell open and Lord Harleston could see that her dress was torn and thick with dust while the shoes on her feet were in tatters.

As if he followed the direction of Lord Harleston's eyes, Brooker explained,

"Her's bin walkin' for miles and were half-dead with hunger and thirst. We fed her and her fell asleep in the back of the wagon and hasn't moved since."

"And you say that her father and mother were killed by the Indians?"

"Yeah, her told us that they'd stopped to cook a meal and she'd gone up the side of the mountain to find water,"

Brooker replied. "The Indians swooped on 'em and there was nothin' her could do but watch."

"Poor little devil!" Jennie said. "It must have been a terrible shock."

"Her didn't tell us much, but you know what happens when the Indians attack."

"We sure do," one of the other cowboys piped up. "And there's trouble the other side of the mountains from all we hears."

"I've heard that too," Jennie said. "You boys take care of yourselves. Will you have a drink on the house? There's nothing else, unless you can pay for it."

"Aw, come on, Jennie, be a bit more generous than that," Brooker pleaded.

"I think you should be my guests," Lord Harleston interposed, "as I am grateful to you for bringing this young woman, who may be a member of my family, to safety."

He handed Brooker a one hundred dollar bill and after one startled glance at it the cowboy's big fist closed over it compulsively and he smiled through his blackened teeth,

"That's mighty generous of you, mister. Thanks a lot. We'll sure make a night of it now we can afford to do so."

Jennie smiled at him.

"You know where to go."

With obvious delight they filed out of the bedroom.

When they had gone, Jennie looked at Lord Harleston.

"I meant what I said," he said in answer to the question in her eyes. "If this is Nelda Harle, then she is my responsibility."

Jennie smiled.

"If you recall, my Lord, thatshe was a present for *me*!"

"I understand," Lord Harleston said, "and, of course, I must compensate you for your loss."

From being a proficient entertainer Jennie became in the flash of a second a hard-dealing businesswoman.

She began by asking a ridiculous price for what she considered 'her property' and in the end accepted less than half of what she pretended to consider was her rightful due but was undoubtedly delighted to receive so much.

Only when she finally capitulated and accepted with a glint in her eyes the dollars that Lord Harleston gave her did he say somewhat ruefully to Waldo,

"I hope I am not presuming on your hospitality by taking this young woman back with me?"

"Of course not," Waldo answered, "and the carriage is outside."

"Do you want me to wake her?" Jennie now asked.

"Let her sleep," Lord Harleston said. "I can tell by the condition of her shoes that the cowboys were not exaggerating when they said that she had walked a really long way."

"What do you intend to do with her?" Jennie enquired.

"I will have to take her back to England," Lord Harleston said in a hard voice, "and hand her over to my relations."

The way he spoke made Jennie glance at him with curiosity before she commented,

"You don't sound particularly pleased at the prospect."

"I can assure you that it is something I find damnably annoying. I have no wish to become encumbered with a woman at this moment, but, knowing who she is, I can hardly leave her here."

It struck him as he spoke that it would have been much more convenient if he had not been present when the cowboys brought her to Jennie as an alternative to being an orphan on the charity of the City Fathers.

Then he was ashamed of himself.

After all, even though she might be Handsome Harry's daughter, she was still a Harle and he knew that he could not have it on his conscience that he had neglected to help a member of the family in distress.

'God knows what I am letting myself in for,' he murmured to himself.

"Shall I carry her to the carriage for you, my Lord?" Waldo asked.

There was something about the way the young man spoke that made Lord Harleston aware that he had not missed the fact that Nelda was extremely pretty.

"Thank you," he nodded, "or perhaps one of the servants can do it."

"I'll do it."

Waldo picked Nelda up in a way that told Lord Harleston that she was very light. She did not move and was obviously in the deep dreamless sleep of complete and utter exhaustion.

Taking her to the bedroom door, Waldo carried her through it.

A servant opened the front door and, as Waldo went out to where the carriage was waiting, Jennie put her hand on Lord Harleston's arm.

"I look forward to seeing you tomorrow night," she said in a caressing voice, "and I'll be ever so disappointed if you don't turn up."

"You are very kind," he responded automatically. "And you're exceedingly good-looking!" she retorted. She bent forward as she spoke and kissed his cheek. "*Au revoir*," she smiled as he moved away.

CHAPTER FOUR

Lord Harleston awoke in a bad temper.

He had slept well, but the moment he came back to consciousness he was acutely aware of the responsibilities that he had taken on the night before and that he was now encumbered with Handsome Harry's daughter.

He thought to himself cynically that she was doubtless like her father and would be a problem to whoever had to look after her.

He was quite determined that once he had taken her back to England that would not be himself and again he was wishing that he had not been in Jennie Rogers's house when she arrived.

At the same time everything decent within himself revolted at the idea of any girl, however disreputable her father might be, being incarcerated in a house of pleasure and she did not look old enough to know that once she had started on the downhill path there was no way back.

He was well aware that charming and certainly attractive though Jennie Rogers looked on the surface, she would not have been a successful madam if she did not rule her house and its occupants with a rod of iron.

The rules were the same the world over, once a girl had become what was to all intents and purposes the property of a madam she could seldom leave or start a different life.

There were, of course, sometimes men who paid for a girl's freedom and even, if they were foolish enough, married a woman from a brothel.

But inevitably, when respectability became disenchanting, they drifted back to their own profession because it was more amusing.

Because he had been so angry at what had happened, he had hardly looked at Nelda, except to notice her dishevelled appearance when they had laid her down on the bed.

That the cowboys were impressed by her looks was no criterion from Lord Harleston's point of view and he wondered how uncouth and uncivilised she might have become in view of the life her father led in gambling halls and mining camps.

Then he remembered, as if he wished to reassure himself, that her mother had been a lady and he remembered his own father speaking to her family about her with approval.

Thinking back into the past when he was quite a small boy he could hear his mother say,

"I am so sorry for the Marlowes. It is not only the scandal of their daughter running away just before she was to be married but that the man she went with was Harry."

"There I agree with you," her husband had replied. "Harry is a disgrace to our family, and I can only hope in all sincerity that, having left this country, he never comes back."

Lady Harleston was, however, not really thinking of Harry for she like all women could not help secretly admiring him, but the girl who had loved him enough to forsake everything that was familiar.

"But he has such charm," she said almost as if she had spoken to herself.

Her husband had given a laugh that had little humour in it.

"Harold can coax gold out of a stone," he remarked, "and he will survive. But the food they eat will be bought by his ill-gotten gains at the card tables."

Lord Harleston remembered joining in the conversation by asking,

"Is Cousin Harry a very good card player, Papa?"

"Far too good!" his father had replied sharply. "And I refuse to speak about him again."

Thinking it over Lord Harleston now remembered that nobody ever spoke of his cousin Harry without referring first to his good looks and then to the fact that wherever there was gambling he would be there.

'And what about the girl?' Lord Harleston asked himself now. 'Perhaps she has the same sleight of hand as her father.'

When he went downstairs to breakfast and found that he was alone and there was no sign of Waldo, he continued pondering on what he could do about Nelda.

He decided after some thought that he must get rid of her as soon as possible.

When he returned to New York, he would pay some respectable woman to take her across the Atlantic to an obliging member of the family who would look after her until he returned.

He wondered what her age was and thought from the quick glimpse he had had of her that she must be in her early teens.

Perhaps he could send her to school and he thought that Mr. Watson could find the name of a strict Seminary for young ladies.

Then it struck him that, if she was as badly behaved as her father, the school might refuse to keep her and that would certainly cause a great deal of unpleasant gossip and speculation.

Everything he thought about her seemed to produce new and intractable problems and he pushed aside the food that he had been eating as he was suddenly finding it tasteless.

He was just helping himself to a second cup of coffee when Waldo came into the room.

"I apologise for being late," he began, "but I did not get to bed until dawn."

"I hope you enjoyed yourself," Lord Harleston replied, trying to keep the sarcastic note from his voice.

"It got rather rowdy after you left," Waldo admitted, "and I don't think you'd have enjoyed the dancing. Those cowboys you gave so much cash to tried to wreck the place before they left."

"I imagine that annoyed Jennie Rogers," Lord Harleston remarked.

"Aw, she can handle them. Wild horses and wild men are all the same to Jennie!"

He spoke with such a note of admiration in his voice that Lord Harleston smiled.

"She's hoping you'll call in and see her again tonight," Waldo told him. "But there are other places I can show you if you are interested."

"I think quite frankly," Lord Harleston answered, "I would rather be on my way to your Ranch to meet your father. As you know, I have really come here to see the cattle."

"Of course," Waldo agreed. "In which case, if we leave in about two hours' time, we can reach the Ranch before dark."

Lord Harleston heard the word '*we*'.

Then he hesitated.

"I am just wondering what I can do about that young woman I brought here last night."

"She can come with us," Waldo suggested, helping himself to an array of dishes on a side table.

"I hope your father and mother will not object to an uninvited guest."

Waldo laughed.

"It's something that is always happening to us. People turn up."

"So I have noticed," Lord Harleston commented.

"Well, I promise you, there's always a spare bed in any house my father owns."

Lord Harleston thought for a moment.

Then he said,

"It has just occurred to me that the girl I brought here last night has no luggage and no clothes."

Waldo sat down at the table, his plate heaped high with eggs and thick pieces of ham.

"That's no problem," he said airily. "I've already told the servants she can borrow anything that belongs to my sister. I should imagine they're somewhere about the same size."

It struck Lord Harleston that in this part of the world people had a generosity and a kindness that in the same circumstances might not be so evident in England.

Aloud he answered,

"I am very grateful, but, of course, since I have made myself responsible for this girl I must provide her with anything she needs."

"Don't worry, my Lord, my mother'll see to all that for you."

Again Lord Harleston could only murmur that it was very kind and listen to his young host as he talked enthusiastically of the gaieties that had occurred after he had left Jennie Rogers's house.

He was just thinking that he should warn Portman that they were leaving when the door opened and Nelda Harle came into the dining room.

She was, now that he could see her properly, very different from the way that she had appeared last night wrapped in a dirty blanket in the cowboys' arms.

To begin with she was taller than she had seemed then and with her hair neatly arranged instead of falling over her shoulders, she was obviously older than Lord Harleston had first reckoned.

With her eyes closed she had looked beautiful, very young and doll-like.

Now he saw that her whole face was dominated by her eyes, which were not the pale blue of a doll but the grey of a troubled sea and they gave her a more serious and certainly more striking look than he had expected.

She was dressed in a gown of spring green silk that threw into prominence the whiteness of her skin.

He noticed too that the ghastly experience that she had passed through and the resulting exhaustion had left shadowy lines under her eyes and she appeared somewhat fragile.

She stood for a moment just inside the doorway as the two men rose to their feet.

Then Nelda stammered,

"I-I was told to come down – here to – see you."

"I hoped you were going to do so," Waldo replied. "As you were asleep when we first saw you, we must introduce ourselves. I'm Waldo Altman Junior and this is my father's house where you're staying."

"That is what – I was told," Nelda said, "and it is very kind of you – to have me here."

She spoke in a low and surprisingly musical voice and Lord Harleston thought with relief that at least, while she had been living in this country, she had not acquired an American accent.

"And this," Waldo went on with a gesture of his hand, "is your relative, Lord Harleston."

As Nelda turned her head to look at him, he saw her grey eyes widen in surprise.

Then she asked,

"Did you say – Lord Harleston?"

"Yes, that is my name," he replied, "and, as I understand your father was Harold Harle, you are a relative of mine."

There was a sudden light in her eyes as she exclaimed,

"Papa often talked – of your father. You must now be Head of the Family."

Lord Harleston inclined his head to acknowledge this and Waldo suggested eagerly,

"Come and sit down and tell us about yourself. Have you had breakfast?"

"Yes, thank you," Nelda replied. "It was brought to me in my room and I must also thank you – for the clothes I am wearing. I am afraid mine are – in rags."

She sat down in the chair that Waldo held for her. Then he and Lord Harleston sat too, while Lord Harleston, crossing his legs and leaning back in the chair, scrutinised Nelda and tried to make up his mind what she was like.

"I'm afraid you've had a terrible time," Waldo said sympathetically. "I don't expect you want to talk about it?"

There was a little pause before Nelda replied with an obvious effort at self-control,

"It – it was horrible – ghastly – and if I had not climbed over the rocks in search of water – they would have k-killed me too."

"You had a lucky escape. The Indians on the plains have been quiet lately and there's been no trouble, so I am sure that your father did not anticipate that it would be dangerous to drive here unaccompanied."

There was a little pause before Nelda responded,

"Somebody did suggest to Papa that he should wait – until there were some other people travelling to Denver – but he wanted to get Mama to a doctor urgently."

"Your mother was ill?"

"Very ill," Nelda answered, "and, although we could perhaps have travelled in a train for half the journey – the railway has not yet reached Leadville. But Mama seemed comfortable and – everything had gone so well that Papa thought it best to drive on and not – waste time."

She spoke with a helpless little note in her voice that Lord Harleston did not miss.

Then, because he was curious, he asked her,

"What was wrong with your mother?"

"I am not quite certain," Nelda replied. "She had grown weaker and weaker during the – winter and a doctor who was travelling through the town, but who I did not think was very skilled, said that the only thing he could suggest was to take her away from Leadville as soon as possible."

"I cannot imagine that a mining town is at all a suitable place for anyone who is sick," Lord Harleston observed.

"No, it was cold and dirty," Nelda approved, "but Papa was making money there and we – needed it – badly."

"I presume your father was making money at the card tables."

Now there was no disguising the condemnation in Lord Harleston's voice and he saw a flush come into Nelda's cheeks.

As if he too felt embarrassed, Waldo asked,

"Surely I can offer you something? What about a cup of coffee?"

Nelda shook her head.

"No, thank you. I was very hungry and thirsty yesterday before the cowboys found me – but now I think it wise not to eat too much all at once."

"I am sure that is very sensible," Waldo agreed.

He was talking to Nelda in an admiring tone that told Lord Harleston that he thought her attractive.

It flashed through his mind that perhaps his disreputable cousin had found his daughter useful in luring rich men into playing cards with him.

He had not missed the blush that rose to her face and he thought it might be because she was ashamed of her life with her father.

He told himself that it was his business to find out exactly what she was like and what she had done in the past before he made plans for her future.

She was exceedingly pretty or rather 'lovely' was the right word. It was not really surprising when one remembered that no one ever spoke of her father without saying how handsome he was.

Also it went without saying that he would not have run away with Elizabeth Marlowe if she had not been particularly attractive.

Prejudiced though he was initially against Nelda, he could not help admitting that as well as being beautiful she looked ladylike and spoke good English in a cultured manner that he could find no fault with.

"We will have a talk when you are feeling stronger," he proposed. "But if you think you are strong enough for the journey, Mr. Altman and I wish to drive to the Ranch where I am to meet his father and mother."

There was silence before Nelda asked,

"Does that – mean we are to travel over the – Plains – again?"

"I am afraid it does," Waldo replied, "but I promise you will be quite safe with us. My father has ordered a number of items to be taken out to the Ranch and, as you've had trouble with the Arapahos, we'll take not only the wagons but several men on horseback with us."

"I-I will – try not to be – frightened," Nelda said in a brave little voice.

"I'll look after you," Waldo offered impulsively.

Then, as if he felt that he had been too familiar, he looked at Lord Harleston and said,

"And, of course, you and I will carry pistols."

"I am glad you reminded me," Lord Harleston replied. "I have one in my trunk, but I did not expect to need it in Denver."

"The Arapaho and the Cheyenne, who are the Indians of the Plains," Waldo explained, "have been quiet for a long time, but I expect they've heard of the trouble with the Utes on the other side of the Rockies and it's very likely to upset them."

"How can they know about it?" Lord Harleston asked. "I cannot believe that the tribes write to each other!"

Waldo laughed.

"Nothing as civilised as that. The Indians communicate either by drums or by smoke or else, as my mother always says, by thought."

Lord Harleston looked sceptical and he added,

"If you live in this country long enough, you will find that news travels on the wind and the Indians, the Africans and the Chinese always know what's going on long before the white man gets to hear of it!"

"That is true," Nelda agreed, "and I cannot help thinking that if – we could have afforded to take our servant with us – he might have – warned Papa before the – Indians appeared."

Now there was a tremor in her voice and something suspiciously like a sob.

Lord Harleston pushed back his chair.

"I think, if we are leaving soon," he suggested, "it would be a good idea if somebody bought you some of the things you will require."

Nelda glanced at him for a moment in surprise.

Then she said shyly,

"I-I am – afraid I have – no money."

"I am aware of that," Lord Harleston answered, "and, as your Guardian, which is what I am at this moment, I am prepared to pay for anything you need. Here is some money to start with. Come to me if you need any more."

He took some green dollar notes from his pocket and put them down on the table in front of her.

She looked at them and he had a strange feeling that she did not wish to touch them.

Then she picked them up, rose to her feet and said,

"Thank you – thank you very – much, my Lord. I cannot promise to – repay you, although it is what I would like to do."

"There is no need for that. When we have more time, we will talk about your future, but for the moment just leave everything to me."

"Thank – you," Nelda murmured again and quickly went from the room.

Waldo lingered behind for a moment to say to Lord Harleston,

"As I told you last night, my Lord, you're on a winning streak."

He grinned as he spoke, but Lord Harleston did not smile back.

Instead, still in a bad mood, he went upstairs to find Portman and tell him of their plans to visit the Ranch.

There was no point in taking all his clothes, especially those he wore in New York, to a Ranch in the middle of the Prairies when with Nelda on his hands he would have to return to Denver before he could go anywhere else.

Anyway he had no intention of staying very long.

'Once she is on her way to England,' he thought, 'I can then decide what other parts of America I would like to visit.'

He had immediately decided that he had no intention of travelling with a young girl, knowing that because she was pretty it might cause uncomfortable gossip. In any case he had no inclination of being cluttered with a woman, any woman, at this particular moment in his life.

He thought that perhaps Mrs. Altman would be able to advise him how to find a suitable chaperone. And then he decided that the most suitable person would be Mrs. Vanderbilt herself.

But he was reluctant to use her services knowing that, once he was back in New York, she would try to lionise him as she had done before he left for Denver.

'*Damn the girl*, she is a nuisance already!' he mused.

Because he was so eager to be rid of Nelda, he instructed Portman to take only the minimum amount of his luggage to the Ranch, thinking that two nights there would be quite sufficient.

Then he would return to New York, put Nelda on a ship to England and start off on his travels a free man.

Having given Portman his orders, he changed again into his breeches and riding boots, which he thought looked more suitable for a Ranch, and then hurried down the stairs in search of Waldo.

Instead he found Nelda waiting for him in one of the large over-furnished sitting rooms that appeared to be a cross between a Museum and Jennie Rogers's parlour.

Nelda was now wearing a light cape over her green gown and a pretty bonnet trimmed with ribbons of the same colour that tied under her chin.

She rose from the chair where she had been sitting as Lord Harleston entered the room and he saw that she had a book in her hand.

"Are you a reader?" he asked as he glanced at it.

"There are so many books here," she said in a rapt voice. "I wish I could stay longer – so that I could read them all."

"You sound as if books are a treat for you," Lord Harleston remarked.

"Mama and I used to scour for books wherever we were staying," Nelda answered simply, "but as you can imagine – they are hard to find in mining towns and places like that."

Lord Harleston felt inclined to say, 'places where you should not have gone', but he thought that it would be unnecessarily rude and so he merely nodded his head.

"Of course we always travelled with a – great number of books of our own," Nelda went on, "all our favourites which we read over and over again. But when I see shelves and shelves of books like these here, I feel like a starving man – who suddenly sees an enormous meal in front of him."

She gave a little smile as she spoke and Lord Harleston noticed that she had two dimples, one on each side of her mouth.

He had the idea, although he was too polite to say so, that the Altmans had bought the books that furnished the walls in this particular room more because they were decorative than because they had any literary value.

He glanced at the book that Nelda held in her hand and asked,

"What are you reading?"

"It is *Le Prince* by Balzac," she replied.

To Lord Harleston's surprise he saw that it was in French.

"Can you read French?" he asked her.

"Yes, of course. Mama was very insistent that I should speak languages fluently and strangely enough I have found it very useful in some of the places we have stayed."

She saw that Lord Harleston looked puzzled and she explained,

"In a gold rush men of every nation catch the fever, but some of them find it almost impossible to make the Americans understand what they need."

Lord Harleston stiffened.

"Are you telling me that your father actually allowed you to go to the Casinos and Clubs where he played cards? It's unbelievable!"

As he spoke, he thought that it was only what he had expected. But he was appalled at learning the truth, knowing how her respectable relatives in England would be shocked to the core at the very idea.

To his surprise Nelda drew herself up so that she seemed even taller than she actually was and her grey eyes looked at him with what he thought was a spark of anger in them.

She did not speak for a moment and then she said,

"Papa always told me that his relatives disapproved of him and – I fear, my Lord, you are thinking about my father in a way that is most unkind and would distress Mama very much if – she was – here."

This was a reaction that Lord Harleston had not expected and, because he felt that her loyalty in defence of her father was somehow rather touching, he said quickly,

"Forgive me. It is not something that we need discuss at the moment, especially when you have been through such a terrible experience in the last few days."

He thought from the expression on Nelda's face that she did not accept his apology and he was about to say something further when at that moment Waldo came into the room to exclaim,

"Everything is arranged, so we can go, if you are ready."

"We are ready," Lord Harleston confirmed.

But Waldo was looking at Nelda.

"You are quite certain it'll not be too much for you?" he asked her. "If it is, we can quite easily wait another day."

"No, no. I have no wish to be a – nuisance when you have been so kind to me already."

She spoke to Waldo, Lord Harleston noticed, in a very different voice from the one she had used to him and he reflected that he had been somewhat tactless in letting her know so soon how much he disapproved of her father.

"Come on then," Waldo urged them, "everything is out in the yard behind the house."

He led the way and Lord Harleston saw that in the large yard there were congregated three huge covered wagons that were obviously loaded with goods.

They were drawn by four horses each and there was also a comfortable closed carriage on top of which was a pile of luggage.

It was obvious that Waldo was not thinking only of Lord Harleston.

"I thought you would find it rather confined to travel in a closed carriage, so I ordered it for Nelda in case she was tired and wished to sleep. But I thought that to start with she can drive with you and see some of the country."

This was certainly what Lord Harleston wanted and he saw with pleasure that there was a very smart trap with four spirited-looking horses between the shafts.

"These are the best we can offer you," Waldo said, watching his face as he inspected them, "and you will find that they will carry you at a good pace."

Lord Harleston looked at the trap and noted that it had only two comfortable cushioned seats in front and, as if Waldo could read his thoughts, he explained,

"I am going to ride, but I'll change places with you if you become tired of driving."

"Thank you," Lord Harleston smiled. "You think of everything."

"I try to," Waldo replied. "Now, if you're ready, we can start."

He gave the order to one of the men riding a horse who shouted for the wagons to start rolling.

Then Waldo helped Nelda up into the front seat of the trap and Lord Harleston took the reins and followed.

He enjoyed driving the four-in-hand and found that, as the trap was very light and the horses fresh, they proceeded at an excellent speed and on Waldo's instructions quickly moved ahead of the wagons so as to be aay of their dust.

By the time they were out of the City and in open country, Waldo with two other riders as escort and Lord Harleston and Nelda in the trap, were well ahead of the rest of the cavalcade.

The Plains were just as Lord Harleston had expected them to be with grass stretching away into a misty horizon and with clumps of trees and low shrubs scattered to break up the landscape.

As the day was bright and sunny, they now had a splendid view of the snow-capped Rocky Mountains on the other side of the City.

But Lord Harleston was concentrating on his driving, thinking that this was the most interesting thing he had done since he had left England.

Since Nelda did not speak, he wondered if she was still angry with him for criticising her father and then decided that she was.

He glanced at her as she sat beside him and could not help realising that her profile with its straight little nose, perfectly curved lips and small pointed chin silhouetted against the vivid blue of the sky was extraordinarily beautiful.

He told himself sourly that beautiful women were always a nuisance and caused trouble wherever they went.

At the same time it was traditional in the Harle family that there should be beautiful womenfolk, as well as handsome men, and Nelda would certainly not let their name down in that particular.

He found himself wondering how he could explain her background outside the family to people who would inevitably be curious.

The trouble was that Handsome Harry was the type of man who attracted gossip and curiosity wherever he went and those who had once known him, even though he had not been in England for nineteen years, or was it twenty, had never forgotten him.

Besides which the Harle family as a whole had an irritating habit of what Lord Harleston called 'keeping tabs' on all their relatives, good, bad or indifferent.

Because Handsome Harry had been not only an adventurer but an irresistible Casanova where women were concerned, nothing about his youthful escapades had ever been forgotten.

On one particular Lord Harleston was determined, that no one should ever know that he had bought Nelda with actual cash from a madam in a house of pleasure.

If it was even whispered about, he knew that it would damn her completely from a Society point of view and give the men who met her an entirely wrong idea of what they might expect from her in the future.

'She will have to behave herself,' he thought savagely.

He realised, as he thought about it, that, because she looked young and innocent and at the same time so lovely, she would attract men irresistibly without any additional factors.

The trap had gone some distance before Nelda said in a low voice,

"Perhaps – you would rather I – went in the coach? I am quite – ready to do so – if that is your wish."

Lord Harleston looked at her sharply.

"Are you telling me in a somewhat roundabout manner that you are tired? " he asked.

"I am – tired," Nelda admitted, "but I would much rather be in the open air – but not – if it upsets you."

"Why should you think it upsets me?" he asked her bluntly.

"Because I feel that you – resent my being here and – hate me," Nelda replied.

Lord Harleston was so surprised that he turned to look at her as if he could not believe what he had heard.

"Why do you say that?" he asked in amazement.

"Mama would say that I was like the Indians – picking up the vibrations on the air without any need to – hear the drums."

Lord Harleston knew exactly what she meant and felt somewhat ashamed.

"You must understand that I am very worried about you," he said somewhat lamely after a moment.

"There is no need – I don't wish to – upset you and perhaps, if it is possible for me to – return to England, I could ask Mama's family to – look after me."

Lord Harleston realised that he had not considered sending Nelda to the Marlowes.

"I expect your mother knew," he said after a pause, "that your grandfather was so angry with her for running away that he never spoke of her again?"

"Yes, Mama did know and it made her very unhappy. But she said that she loved Papa so much that nothing in the world mattered except for him."

Nelda spoke quite simply in a way that was rather moving.

It flashed through Lord Harleston's mind that any man would feel flattered knowing that a woman cared so much for him that she would sacrifice her home and her family and live a life that at times must have been intolerably stressful and perhaps humiliating.

Aloud he said,

"There must be members of your family who I am certain would wish to get to know you and perhaps welcome you, but as a Harle you are my responsibility."

"B-but – as you – hated Papa – I thought I would rather – live with Mama's family."

"I did not say that I hated your father," Lord Harleston corrected her quickly.

Nelda did not reply, but he knew that she was thinking that he had revealed his feelings by the way he spoke and the tone of his voice.

He also had the uncomfortable feeling that she could read his thoughts and then he told himself that he was being imaginative and, of course, she could do nothing of the sort.

Because he wished now to be conciliatory, he carried on,

"You will understand that I have not met your father since I was very young and I only heard about him intermittently over the years while he was living abroad. What I want you to do when we can be alone is to tell me about your life and, of course, about yourself."

"Perhaps it is best for you not to – know about it, my Lord," Nelda said quietly.

"Why should you say that?"

"Because you are bound to – disapprove of Papa and, as I loved him – anything you might say – against him would make me angry and unhappy."

She spoke softly and yet there was a little hint of steel behind the words that astonished Lord Harleston.

"I promise you that if you tell me about your father I will listen to anything you have to say with an open mind and I will certainly not sit in judgement on him now that he is dead."

"Yes – he is – d-dead," Nelda repeated almost beneath her breath, "but I find it hard to believe. He was always so – full of life and made everything – even the most difficult situations – seem funny and – somehow an adventure."

Her voice broke and she turned her head away from Lord Harleston and he knew that it was because she was hiding her tears.

He then suddenly thought that he had been unforgivably brutal to someone so small and vulnerable.

It was almost as if he had been unsportsmanlike and he knew that it was because he was ignoring the terrible experience that she had just passed through.

He had been thinking not of her but of himself and the problems she presented to him rather than trying to understand what she must be suffering.

He took his left hand from the reins to lay it on hers.

"Forgive me, Nelda, and let us start again from the beginning. I think we have started off on the wrong foot and that is a mistake. We have to work together to plan your future and make it as happy as possible."

Any of the ladies who had lost their hearts to Lord Harleston could have told Nelda that when he spoke like that in a particularly beguiling voice he was irresistible.

Lord Harleston felt Nelda's hand quiver beneath his and, when she was free of his touch, she turned her face to say,

"If I was – rude – please forgive me."

"There is nothing for you to forgive. Perhaps we are both a little on edge, which is not surprising."

"N-no – of course not," Nelda agreed, "and I am trying to – thank you for being – so kind to me."

He smiled at her and again it was something that women found exceedingly attractive.

They drove on and an hour later Waldo called a halt while they ate a luxurious midday meal.

The wagons formed a circle in the traditional manner that Lord Harleston had read about in books and noted with interest.

They did not picnic on the ground, but a table and chairs were brought from one of the wagons and a very substantial luncheon was provided in large hampers.

As Portman was there to serve them, it was quite a feast.

They drove on after luncheon, stopping only to water the horses at one of the many rivers on the Plain.

Waldo told them that there had been plenty of rain recently, but later the rivers would become nothing more than streams and the lakes would even dry up into muddy swamps.

Now they were beginning to have glimpses of herds of cattle grazing on the grass. Waldo pointed out that the cattle Empires all had their own particular brand marks, but he had not yet seen any of those belonging to the Prairie Cattle Company.

It was beautiful country, at the same time very vast, and they seemed to be going further and further away from anything civilised into an indeterminate landscape where human beings had not yet ventured.

Nelda was very quiet and Lord Harleston sensed that she was still very tired. However he realised that, although they had suggested it several times, she had no wish to travel alone in the closed carriage.

With a perception that he did not usually possess he was aware, although she did not say so, that she only felt safe when she was close to him and when they were not too far ahead of the wagons. He therefore deliberately did not push the horses.

At about four o'clock in the afternoon Waldo came up alongside them to say,

"The Ranch is less than four hours' drive ahead. Would you like to ride now?"

Lord Harleston was just about to say that there was nothing he would like more when he realised that Nelda had made an involuntary little gesture with her hand towards him as if she pleaded with him without words not to leave her.

For a moment he hesitated as to what he should do.

Then, making a decision that really surprised himself, he said,

"I am enjoying driving these horses, but you go ahead, if you want to."

"You can give them their heads now. We are on our own grazing lands so and are quite safe."

He took a long look at Nelda before he added,

"I'll tell Pa and Ma to kill the fatted calf by the time you arrive. So long for now!"

He spurred his horse as he spoke and galloped off leaving a cloud of dust in his wake.

Lord Harleston and Nelda had travelled for another mile before they saw a small stream beside some trees and Nelda asked,

"Do you think the horses are thirsty? Perhaps we should let them drink?"

"A good idea," Lord Harleston answered.

He turned the trap as he spoke towards the stream, which was winding through the trees and bushes in a very attractive manner.

He drove the leading horses into the stream so that the others would reach the water and as they did so Nelda jumped down from the trap saying,

"I feel so dusty that I want to wash my hands and face."

Lord Harleston could understand why she was anxious to do so.

The dust they had encountered on their journey had left a film over the horses. It was half an inch thick on the floor of the trap and his clothes were covered in it.

He took off his hat and shook it and saw how much dust had accumulated on it.

Nelda knelt down beside the stream and pulled off her bonnet and washed her face in the clear water.

"It's lovely and cool," she exclaimed.

Lord Harleston realised that the horses would not wander away while they were drinking and so he fixed the reins to the buckboard and climbed down too.

As Nelda had said, the water was very cool and, as he washed his face and his hands, he thought that the one thing he would enjoy on arrival at the Ranch would be a bath.

Nelda rose from where she was kneeling and wiped her face with a small handkerchief.

Lord Harleston smiled.

"I should have thought of it before. My handkerchief is certainly larger than yours."

He handed her one from his breast pocket that had been neatly folded by Portman.

She took it from him, wiped her face and her hands and then handed it back to him.

"Thank you. I feel much fresher now. I should have remembered the dust on the Prairie and brought a towel."

Lord Harleston recalled how dusty and dirty she had been last night when the cowboys had carried her into Jennie Rogers's house.

He knew that she was thinking of it too as she turned to look back at the way they had come.

Then suddenly she gave a shrill cry of fear.

"Indians!" she called out in a voice that seemed to be strangled in her throat. "*Indians!*"

CHAPTER FIVE

Startled, Lord Harleston looked in the direction she was pointing.

Far away on the horizon was a long line that appeared to be coming nearer and behind it a cloud of dust.

He glanced quickly in the direction of the wagons and realised that, while they had been watching the horses and washing, the wagons had moved on quite a considerable way from them.

He put out his hand towards the trap and, almost as if they sensed that something was wrong, the horses put their heads up and were already beginning to move out of the water and in the direction of the other horses.

Lord Harleston would have stopped them, but Nelda said with a cry,

"We must hide! Our only – hope is to – hide."

Without saying anything more she sprang as lithely as a young gazelle over the stream onto the bank on the other side and then she was running frantically between the trees.

There was nothing that Lord Harleston could do but follow her and, as he too jumped the stream, he wondered if they were courting certain death or whether to join the others might be even more hazardous.

He had thought from his first look at the Indians that there must be a great number of them.

As he ran after Nelda, who was moving with the swiftness of fear ahead of him, he calculated that with three men in each wagon and four on horseback, that was sixteen guns not counting Portman, who could use one quite effectively.

'We should have stayed together,' he thought.

He knew that by stopping to drink at the stream on Nelda's suggestion they had now separated themselves irretrievably from the wagons.

He ran on and now he could hear the sound of hoofs, at first like the faint roar of distant waves and then growing louder and louder.

He wondered if those in the wagons had been alerted and were already forming the traditional circle so that they could fire at the enemy behind the shelter of the vehicles.

All he could do was to concentrate on catching up with Nelda, who he was aware was running from the shelter of one tree to another. Fortunately they were thicker here than anywhere else they had seen on the Prairie.

Suddenly there were ear-splitting yells of the Indians' war cries, followed rapidly by a fusillade of shots.

It was then that Nelda stopped and, as Lord Harleston reached her, he realised that she had run until she was exhausted and was gasping for breath in a way which told him that she was near to collapse.

He put his arms around her to stop her from falling down and she laid her head against his shoulder, her breath coming intermittently and her whole body trembling.

Lord Harleston could only hold her and listen to the war cries and sound of shots, which seemed to intensify.

He guessed that the Indians were now in their usual manner firing as they rode round and round the wagons, heedless of the toll that it took of their own warriors.

'How could I have imagined that this could ever happen to me?' he worried.

He knew that it would indeed be a miracle if he and Nelda escaped being killed.

She was now finding it not so hard to breathe, but, because her body had become stiff, he knew that she was listening and was aware even more vividly than he was of what was occurring because she had seen it happen before.

After what seemed an interminable time, there were no more shots and the war cries died away into an uneasy silence.

Nelda did not relax and Lord Harleston knew from what he had read that this was the moment when the Indians, having killed their victims, would scalp them.

They would then take every possession they required from the dead bodies and from the wagons before riding away with the spoils.

He was aware, simply because she did not move or speak, that Nelda also knew what was happening and they both waited, listening until the very effort was a physical pain.

Then so suddenly that they both jumped, the war cries came again, there was the thunder of hoofs passing them and gathering speed until they faded away into the distance when finally nothing more could be heard.

It was then, realising that they were both alive and had for the moment nothing more to fear, that Lord Harleston drew in his breath, which he did not realise he had been holding.

"It's all over," he said in a voice that did not sound like his own.

He felt the stiffness go out of Nelda's body and she burst into tears.

She cried tempestuously as a child might and Lord Harleston was aware that it was because she had kept herself so strictly under control after the death of her father and mother.

Now her pent-up emotions broke from the bonds she had placed on them and she cried until it swept away thought and will power.

"It's all right," he kept saying, "it's all right. They have gone!"

He tried to pat her shoulder and as he did so realised that when she had been running she had lost the pins that kept her hair in place.

Now it fell over her shoulders as it had done the night the cowboys had brought her to Jennie Rogers's house.

As he touched it, he realised in some obscure corner of his mind that it was as soft as silk, softer than any woman's hair that he had ever touched before.

But his brain was preoccupied with wondering how they could reach safety before it grew dark.

By now the sun was sinking low on the horizon and he recognised that dusk would fall swiftly.

It would be very frightening when darkness came and the wild animals on the Prairie were on the prowl to be anywhere near the carnage the Indians had left behind them.

Nelda's tears had abated a little and Lord Harleston said,

"You have been very brave up to now, but you do realise that we cannot stay here in case the Indians come back?"

He felt the shudder that went through her as she raised her head to say,

"If – if we go – where can we – hide?"

Her voice was hoarse and tears were still running down her cheeks.

It struck Lord Harleston as he looked at her that she was really lovely, in fact lovelier than any woman he had seen before who had been crying.

"I think as Fate has saved our lives so far, it will help us again," he tried to reassure her.

She drew in her breath.

Then she asked hesitantly so that he could hardly hear,

"Y-you are – sure t-they are – all d-dead?"

"I am afraid so."

He knew that the Indians when scalping their victims would have made certain that there was no life left in them.

He had no wish to see the horrors that had been left behind and it was certainly something that was not for Nelda's eyes.

He took her by the hand and set off in the direction that they had been travelling in before, keeping out of sight of what was left of the wagons, where the men who had escorted them would be lying.

He thought with sadness how he would miss Portman and yet he knew that, as he had been a soldier, he would, if he had the choice, rather die fighting than be pensioned off to live in some alms-house.

He had often talked of his time in the Army.

~101~

"There's an excitement about fightin', my Lord," he had said. "It gives you a thrill you don't get no other way."

Thinking of Portman's grin as he spoke, Lord Harleston could only hope that his death had been a quick one, while he still knew the thrill of battle.

Nelda was now no longer crying and had regained her self-control.

Lord Harleston could not help thinking that, if he had had any other woman of his acquaintance with him, she would have been wailing and fainting with the horror of what had happened.

She would also be making sure that he would think of nothing else but comforting and placating her.

He tightened his grip on Nelda's fingers and felt without her saying so that it comforted her to know that he was there and that she could rely on him.

They walked for a long way, in fact well over a mile before Lord Harleston guessed that they would be out of sight of the wreckage and moved in the direction of the track that they had been following across the Plains, which would eventually lead them to the Ranch.

He knew that when they did not arrive Waldo would be worried and doubtless send people to search for them.

He had the feeling, however, that might not happen until after dark and he was becoming apprehensive about spending the night in the open with Nelda.

He had his pistol in his pocket, which was some consolation and he had known when he was listening to the Indians' war cries that, if they were discovered, he would have to shoot Nelda rather than allow her to be captured.

What his own fate would be was obvious.

But sometimes the Indians took white women away with them and to allow that to happen to any woman he was with was unthinkable.

They walked on and now it was dusk. The last vestige of light from the sun had vanished and the stars were beginning to glitter overhead.

Just as Lord Harleston was wondering desperately what he could do, he saw in the distance an enclosure and thought that they must be in the vicinity of a farm.

A short time later set back amongst some trees, he could discern a roof.

As they went through an open five-bar gate, Lord Harleston could see in front of him a small farmhouse that was exactly like those he had seen illustrated in the books he had read.

There was a sloping roof, a wooden verandah with steps up to it and on both sides enclosures for animals and a few sheds.

Nelda spoke after a long silence.

"A house!" she exclaimed. "At least we can have a roof over our heads until morning."

"That is just what I was thinking," Lord Harleston replied. "Again we have been very fortunate, Nelda, I think the Gods are looking after us."

"I-I was – praying," she said softly.

They walked on and, as they neared the house, Lord Harleston thought it strange that there were no animals to be seen or heard.

There surely should have been cows, calves and perhaps pigs in some of the enclosures and certainly chickens.

They might, of course, have been shut up for the night, but still he felt uneasy and, releasing Nelda's hand, he drew his pistol from his pocket.

"What – is the – matter?" she asked in a frightened voice. "What do you – suspect?"

"I am just taking sensible precautions," Lord Harleston replied.

He approached the house cautiously and then saw, when he had almost reached the verandah, that the front door was open.

It struck him that perhaps the owners had run away to hide because they had heard the Indians coming, but it was unlikely that they would have taken their animals with them and he suspected that the Indians had raided this farm and taken away the livestock.

If they had, everything was now very quiet and there appeared to be nobody about, neither white man nor Indian.

Stepping ahead of Nelda, pistol in hand, Lord Harleston walked up the first step of the verandah and as he did so he called out,

"Is there anyone at home?"

There was no answer and his voice seemed to echo back at him almost eerily.

"I think it's all right," he said to Nelda, "but keep behind me."

He crossed the verandah and walked in through the open door.

There was one large room sparsely furnished with a stove at one end and there was a glow from a wood fire, which made it obvious that the house had been recently occupied.

It was, however, difficult to see very clearly as it was darker inside the house than it was outside.

Lord Harleston looked around, saw that there was a door leading to what he supposed was a bedroom on the other side of the house and realised that he must investigate what was there.

He was just about to walk towards it when Nelda gave a shrill scream.

It was so loud and so unexpected that Lord Harleston started, half-turned towards her, and by doing so, saved his life!

Dropping down from a beam in the ceiling came an Indian with a knife in his hand that he intended to drive into Lord Harleston.

Fortunately his movement made the Indian's spring slightly off target and, as he fell against him, Lord Harleston knocked the knife out of his hand, which clattered to the floor.

At the same time the Indian's grip on him prevented him from firing his own pistol and with his other hand he went for Lord Harleston's throat.

Fighting violently, Lord Harleston fell to the ground with the Indian on top of him.

Although he was strong and a good pugilist in ordinary circumstances he was somewhat encumbered by the tightness of his riding coat and the Indian now astride him was attempting to throttle him.

Lord Harleston struggled desperately, but his riding boots slipped on the floor while the Indian fought with his feet as well as his hands.

It flashed through Lord Harleston's mind that this was a fight that he was not going to win.

Then suddenly and completely unexpectedly, as the Indian tightened his hold on his throat, he suddenly slumped forward with a guttural cry that broke the silence that they had been struggling in.

For a moment Lord Harleston could hardly believe that it had happened until he saw the knife embedded in the base of the Indian's neck and the blood already beginning to ooze over his brown skin.

He knew then that it was Nelda who had saved him.

He pushed the man off him, climbed to his feet and without speaking dragged him by the arm out through the open door, across the verandah and onto the dusty ground outside.

He hesitated for a moment and then thought that to leave the body in the open where he could be seen by any of his tribe prowling around in search of him would be a mistake.

Still dragging him by the arm, he moved to where a clump of shrubs and trees afforded shelter for the buildings.

It was nearly dark by now, but, as he pulled the Indian in amongst the thick bushes and undergrowth, Lord Harleston caught sight of something white and as he moved nearer he saw what it was.

A very perfunctory inspection told him that he had been right in thinking that the Indians had visited this homestead and taken away the livestock.

Lying in the bushes were the farmer and his wife and they had both been scalped!

He left the Indian beside them and went back into the house.

Nelda was standing where he had left her and, although he could not see the expression on her face, he knew that there would be a stricken look in her eyes and that she was scared into immobility by the shock of what had just occurred.

"You saved my life, Nelda," he said gently, "and I am very grateful. I think, if we intend to stay here tonight, we must take precautions so that we have no unwelcome visitors."

She did not answer, but he saw that she was listening and he said,

"Let's see if we can find some candles or perhaps an oil lamp. Then we will close the shutters and barricade ourselves in."

The way he spoke made it sound almost like a game and, as if she was a child obeying him, she moved a little helplessly towards the dresser that stood against one wall.

Lord Harleston looked in the other direction and gave an exclamation,

"A lamp! That is what I was hoping for and, if we make a spill, we can light it from the fire."

Nelda, as he had intended, began to look for some paper and then in a strained, hesitating little voice, she said,

"Perhaps it w-would be wise to – close the shutters f-first."

"Of course," Lord Harleston agreed. "It would be very sensible. We don't want anybody to know we are here and, as we also don't wish to be in the dark, perhaps you can poke the fire and make it give enough light for me to see how this lamp works."

He closed the door and, by feeling rather than by seeing, shot the bolt across it and then groped his way to the windows. There were two of them facing onto the verandah and one at the side.

They all had heavy wooden shutters, also with strong bolts attached to hold them in place.

By the time Lord Harleston had closed the third one there was a considerable amount of light coming from the fire.

He saw that Nelda was burning logs that were in a big pile beside the stove and she had also found some old newspapers.

He walked back towards her and she said still in a very small voice that seemed to be forced from her lips,

"I-I have made a – spill for you."

She put it into his hand and he carried the oil lamp near enough to the fire so that he could see how to light it.

It took a little time because it was something that he had never done before.

When finally he had lit it and the whole room seemed to come to life, he felt as pleased with himself as if he had won an arduous race.

"It – it makes everything – seem better," Nelda remarked looking at the lamp.

"Of course and, in case you are still worried, I am going to explore the rest of the house, although I am sure that there is nobody here but us."

He thought that there was no point in him telling her that he knew where the previous occupants were, but just as a precaution, carrying his pistol in his hand, he opened the bedroom door.

As he expected, it was empty and there were only a few pieces of simple furniture and a large iron bedstead covered with a patchwork quilt and above it a religious text, framed and embroidered in wool.

"At least you will be able to sleep comfortably until Waldo sends a search party to find us," Lord Harleston commented.

"Do you think he will?" Nelda enquired eagerly.

"Naturally, but I don't think we can expect them until morning."

"No – I suppose not."

She looked around the room and asked,

"Are you – hungry? Shall I – try to find you – something to – eat?"

"I think that would be a very good idea. I always believe that things seem better and certainly less frightening than they do on an empty stomach."

Nelda went to the end of the room where there was a rough sink. Lord Harleston suspected that the water for it would have to be brought in from a well outside.

But Nelda found a large ewer on the floor full of water and there was also a kettle and a frying pan.

Then she opened a cupboard and exclaimed,

"There are some eggs and there is no reason why – they should not be fresh."

"I should certainly enjoy eating them," Lord Harleston said. "I presume you can cook?"

"Of course I can and I will make you an omelette unless you would prefer a fried egg."

"I would enjoy an omelette, if it is well made," Lord Harleston replied teasingly.

"I shall be very ashamed if you are disappointed," she answered firmly.

She busied herself preparing the eggs and Lord Harleston took off his coat, which he found had been torn on the shoulder when he was fighting with the Indian.

As he did so, he saw that the sleeve of his white shirt was stained with blood.

He was looking at it in surprise when Nelda glanceded round from her cooking and gave a cry of dismay.

"You are injured! Why did you not tell me?"

"It's only a scratch," he answered, "and I don't even remember it happening."

"The Indian must have struck you with his knife before you knocked it out of his hand."

"And enabled you to save my life," Lord Harleston said quietly.

"I-I thought he was going to – kill you."

"I hate to admit it, but he might have done so, if you had not killed him first."

"I am glad I saved you – but it is – wrong to kill another human being – even an Indian!"

She spoke in a manner that told Lord Harleston that it was really perturbing her and he said quickly,

"While I will admit that to murder anybody is wrong, to kill in order to save a person's life cannot be wrong and that is what you did, Nelda."

"I had to – save you," she said almost as if she justified her action to herself.

"I am very very glad to be alive."

As if she was still seeking reassurance from him, Nelda looked up into his eyes and for a moment she felt as if she could not move.

Then she suggested swiftly as if she was embarrassed,

"I-I must wash your – wound."

"As I have said, it can only be a scratch," Lord Harleston replied.

He undid his cufflink as he spoke and rolled up his sleeve.

During the fight and afterwards when he had been only conscious of the bruising that the Indian had inflicted on his neck, he had not known that there had been any damage done to his arm.

Now, as he saw the long cut that the point of the knife had made as he struck it upwards and out of the Indian's hand, he felt it begin to smart and it was still bleeding.

"Come to the sink and I will wash it," Nelda said insistently. "You never know, but the knife might have been poisoned."

She tipped some water into a small basin.

There was a clean towel by the side of the sink and she dipped this into the water and very gently wiped away the blood.

Then she said,

"I wonder if they have any spirits here. Most farmers drink bourbon."

"Are you suggesting that I need it to stop me from fainting at the sight of my own blood?" Lord Harleston asked.

Nelda smiled and he saw both her dimples.

"It's not for you, but for your arm to be used as a disinfectant. Mama always said it was better than anything we could buy at a pharmacy."

She did not wait for Lord Harleston to comment but went back to the dresser and opened the lower cupboard.

"I have found some!" she cried almost as if it was buried treasure and came back with a bottle of whisky that was half-full.

"I imagine it is what the Indian was looking for," Lord Harleston remarked.

He had read that the white man's spirit was greatly prized amongst the Indian warriors and even a little of it went straight to their heads.

Nelda was not listening. She was soaking a clean piece of cloth with the whisky.

Then she turned and warned him,

"I am afraid this is going to hurt you."

"I will try to be brave," Lord Harleston replied mockingly.

The spirit did indeed sting abominably, but he knew that Nelda was wise in thinking that a wound, however small, inflicted with an Indian's knife should be prevented from festering.

"I must now bandage it," she said, "and while I am looking to see if there is anything in the bedroom I can use, please don't touch it or let it get dirty in any way."

Lord Harleston smiled at the authoritative way she spoke and waited while she hurried to the bedroom.

She came back after some minutes with a long strip of thin white lawn, too fine and too expensive to be the sort of material used by a farmer's wife.

She also had made a pad of the same lawn and he asked,

"Where did you find that? "

Nelda looked a little uncomfortable as she replied,

"I am afraid it comes from the petticoat that I borrowed from Miss Altman, but perhaps she will forgive me in the circumstances."

"You are certainly an expert at coping with accidents," Lord Harleston said as she put the pad on his arm and started to bandage it.

"Mama treated many accidents in the mining camps and she allowed me sometimes to help her."

"I am sure that is something you should not have been doing," Lord Harleston remarked.

He spoke without thinking and wondered once again whether Nelda would be angry with him, but she replied simply,

"They came to our house because they knew that Mama was such an expert and they would sit on the steps outside patiently for hours with blood dripping from cut fingers or with bruised and battered faces. We could hardly let them suffer without doing what we could to help them."

"I should imagine they were grateful."

"Very very grateful. Papa always said it was a disgrace that they did not have proper medical care and doctors in places like Leadville for a great number of people died because there was nobody skilled available to treat them."

"So you and your mother acted as physicians," Lord Harleston observed as if he spoke to himself.

"We could only help people with minor injuries, of course, and Papa made us promise that they would never come inside the house. So they sat on the verandah and when that was full on the ground outside. When Mama grew tired, Papa used to send them away and – it was pathetic when they begged him to allow them to come back the next day."

Lord Harleston did not say anything and once again, as if she read his thoughts, Nelda went on,

"I know you are thinking that Papa should not have taken us to a mining town, but that was where he could make more money than anywhere else. He was saving every penny he could to take Mama to Florida because he thought that a warmer climate – would make her better."

Although he did not wish at this moment to seem curious, Lord Harleston could not help asking,

"Was there no other way that your father could make money?"

He thought as he asked the question that Nelda's eyes would flash at him as they had done before.

But, as she finished tying his bandage, she said with a little smile,

"It was a question Papa said that he asked himself over and over again and he always added,

"'Unfortunately I was brought up to be a gentleman! You may not believe it, my dearest, living in this country, but in England gentlemen are not supposed to work'."

Lord Harleston recognised that this was true and he commented,

"It was your father's own choice to come to America."

"He thought it would be an adventure," Nelda answered, "and also somewhere where he could be with Mama and escape the anger of your family and hers that they had run away together."

"It certainly caused a great deal of criticism at the time."

"They knew that, but how could they help being in love with each other? They were so blissfully happy and nothing else mattered, not even being very – poor."

There was a rapt little expression on Nelda's face as once again she was busying herself preparing the eggs for the omelette.

"So your father made his living by playing cards."

Lord Harleston tried to make it sound like a statement rather than a criticism and, as if he succeeded, Nelda answered,

"Papa said once that it was the only talent the Almighty had given him and we are instructed in the Bible not to bury our talents but to use them."

"Even so, as you have just said, you were sometimes very poor."

"Very – very – poor," Nelda replied, "especially when those who owed Papa money would not pay him."

Lord Harleston thought that must have been a frequent hazard considering the type of people Handsome Harry played against.

Aloud he said,

"That must have been extremely frustrating."

"It was, but Papa was very lucky on the whole, although once he even had to pawn – Mama's Wedding ring when we had nothing else."

She gave a little sigh and added, almost as if she spoke to herself,

"But Papa always made us laugh even in the darkest days. And when things went right, he would come home with his pockets full, fling the money down on the table and then dance around the room with Mama and it always made everything seem so – wonderful!"

The way she spoke was very moving. Then because she had started to recall the past tears came into her eyes and Lord Harleston suggested quickly,

"If you are going to make that omelette now, I will see if there is a loaf of bread in the cupboard and toast some slices by the fire for us."

"That would be very nice," Nelda agreed.

Lord Harleston found a loaf, a knife and also a large pat of newly churned butter, which he supposed had been made from milk from the cows that the Indians must have stolen.

He carried it to the table where the oil lamp was standing, while Nelda put a saucepan on the fire and placed two plates on top of the stove to warm.

Lord Harleston put a slice of bread on the point of the knife and toasted it as he had done when he was a fag at Eton.

He had toasted three slices before Nelda said that the omelette was now ready and placed three quarters of it in front of him.

He ate it appreciatively saying,

"You are quite right. You are a very good cook."

"I can cook quite elaborate dishes when I have the ingredients," Nelda answered, "and, if we have to stay here for a long time, I will try to vary the menu."

"I shall enjoy that, but at the same time, I shall feel relieved when we are rescued."

They both ate in silence until Nelda said as if it had been in her thoughts for some time,

"I-I suppose there was – nothing we could have done to – save the men in the wagons – and your valet?"

"I shall miss Portman," Lord Harleston replied, "but there was nothing we could have done except get killed ourselves and that, you must agree, would have been very foolish."

"At least you would not have had to – bother about me in the – future."

Lord Harleston realised as she spoke that she was still thinking that he hated her and that he had no wish to be responsible for her in any way.

He looked at her across the table and realised that she was very different from what he had originally expected.

In the light from the oil lamp with her fair hair falling over her shoulders as she ate made her look very entrancing and indeed rather like a nymph who had just stepped out of a Fairytale.

"I have not forgotten that you saved my life, Nelda," he said in his deep voice, "and for that I owe you a great debt of gratitude which is going to be very difficult to repay."

"There is no – reason for you to feel like – that. It was just that I thought the Indian was going to – kill you and something – or somebody – outside myself told me what – I must do."

"That was obviously my Guardian Angel, if I have one," Lord Harleston added with a smile, "or perhaps it is you who are that, although I did not realise it when we first met."

He recalled as he spoke how one of the cowboys had said that Nelda looked like an angel and it occurred to him that many a true word was spoken in jest.

Because she was feeling a little embarrassed, Nelda rose to collect the plates from the table.

"Are you still hungry?" she asked. "I can see if there is anything else here that I could cook for you."

"As we had a very large luncheon," Lord Harleston replied, "I have now had everything I need. But may I point out that your kettle is boiling?"

"I thought it would be wiser for us to drink tea rather than water. Mama always said one should never drink the water in a new place unless it had been boiled."

"That is very sensible," Lord Harleston agreed, "and I would appreciate a cup of tea."

Nelda made it for him and, when he was drinking it, she said,

"I am surprised you don't want to drink the whisky, my Lord."

"Why?" he asked. "As a matter of fact it is a drink I really don't like."

"The men here always seem to want whisky, but Papa preferred French wines, which, of course, are almost unprocurable here or else too expensive."

"Sometime you must tell me about the life you led with your father," Lord Harleston said, "but not tonight as I am sure you are tired and should go to bed."

"What about you?"

"I will sleep here in the chair."

"But – that will be – uncomfortable."

"I have slept in far worse places when I was in the Army. The room is warm and safe and we neither of us need to worry about anything until tomorrow morning."

He knew as he spoke that she did not find him very convincing. But with the shutters closed it would be impossible for him to be taken by surprise and he saw too that she was now looking exhausted.

"Go to bed, Nelda," he insisted.

"I found some clean sheets when I was looking for a bandage," Nelda told him. "I am sure if you prefer I could make you up a bed by putting two chairs together."

Lord Harleston smiled.

"Stop worrying about me," he ordered her, "and go to bed now. You have been through quite enough for one day!"

He thought as he spoke it was not just one day but three, which would have reduced any other woman of his acquaintance to complete hysterics.

As if she knew that he was being sensible, Nelda said,

"Goodnight, my Lord – and thank you for – being so kind to – me."

She did not wait for an answer, but went into the bedroom and closed the door.

Lord Harleston heard her moving about and supposed that she must be changing the sheets.

Then he pulled up another chair in front of the one by the stove where he could stretch out his legs and decided to take off his riding boots.

As they had been made especially for him by Maxwell in Dover Street, they were a perfect fit and it was difficult to remove them with no Portman to help him.

But he had walked a long way and he reckoned that if he kept them on all night his feet would feel swollen and sore by the morning.

Accordingly he was determined to take them off and then was relieved to be free of them.

He settled himself in the armchair, his pistol beside him and, having turned down the lamp to only a faint glow, he closed his eyes.

He was just drifting into the comfortable state between sleeping and being just awake when he heard the sound of a door opening.

Instantly he was alert until he realised that it was the bedroom door and then he saw Nelda standing in the opening.

She looked rather like a ghost until he realised that she was wearing a sheet draped around her and the only part of her he could see was her fair hair falling over her shoulders.

"What is the matter, Nelda?"

She stood gazing at him.

Then she said in a very small voice,

"You will – think I am very – f-foolish and I am – ashamed of myself, but because I am – alone in there – I am – f-frightened."

He could see the expression on her face and knew that she was speaking the truth and he felt that beneath the sheet her whole body was trembling.

He smiled reassuringly at her.

"That is understandable and therefore there are only two things we can do. Either you can come and sleep here beside me or I can come and sleep beside you."

"I-I don't want to make you – uncomfortable," Nelda sighed miserably, "but I keep thinking I hear Indians – creeping around outside – and I want to scream!"

"You are safe enough here," Lord Harleston assured her, "and I promise if there are any Indians about I should be aware of it and shoot them before they can force their way into the house."

"I – expect you think I am very foolish," Nelda said with a little sob.

"I think you are the bravest woman I have ever met in my whole life," Lord Harleston answered. "Now you go and get back into bed. I will come and lie beside you."

"Perhaps – Mama would think it – wrong of me to ask you to – do such a thing."

"It is no more wrong," Lord Harleston declared firmly, "than that we should both sit uncomfortably bolt upright on these rather hard chairs all night. And if you want the truth, my legs are already beginning to ache not to mention my arm."

He knew as he spoke that Nelda would worry about him and, as he had anticipated, she said,

"Is your arm – hurting you?"

"It's not bad, but I can feel it throbbing," Lord Harleston admitted.

"I should not have listened to you when you said that you would be all right in the chair. I would have managed much better than you."

"As it is, neither of us is going to manage on a chair," Lord Harleston said firmly, "so go and get into bed, Nelda, and I will carry in the light."

"It was – stupid of me to blow out the candle. Everything seemed so much more – terrifying in the dark."

"I suppose it does, so we will keep the light burning."

He went to the table to pick up the oil lamp and, when he did so, he realised that Nelda had gone back into the bedroom.

Following her he saw that she was now in the bed, still wrapped in the sheet, and she was leaning back against a pillow that she had put a clean pillowslip on.

There was another one beside her that was also spotlessly clean and Lord Harleston placed the lamp on what was to be his side of the bed.

Then he looked around as if to make sure that Nelda's fears were just imaginary.

The window was shut tight and barred and there was just enough light from the fire in the living room to see through the open door that there was no one there to threaten them.

Lord Harleston lay down on top of the bed, pulling the patchwork quilt over him.

"Now go to sleep," he insisted, "and worry about nothing. I am here to protect you and, if anyone disturbs us, I will shoot on sight."

Nelda did not speak for a moment.

Then she asked,

"You are not – angry with me – anymore?"

"I think you are aware without my having to tell you," Lord Harleston replied. "If your intuition is working properly, you would know that I am not only very grateful to you but I think, after what we have been through together, we are friends."

He turned his head on the pillow to look at her as he spoke and saw that she was smiling at him in a way that she not had done before.

"I would – like to be your – friend," she hesitated a little, "because I have – never had one."

"Then as a friend," Lord Harleston replied, "I suggest that you forget everything that has happened and go to sleep."

"I will – try," Nelda replied.

There was silence until she whispered,

"Now you are here I am not frightened anymore and it will be easier to sleep in the dark."

"Of course," Lord Harleston agreed.

He turned down the wick of the lamp and settled himself comfortably.

Then Nelda said very softly,

"I have thanked God that we are – safe and I think, if your Guardian Angel is looking after you – mine is looking after – me."

Lord Harleston smiled.

"I was just wondering," Nelda went on, "what might have happened to me when the cowboys took me to Denver – if they had not given – me to you?"

She paused before she added in a puzzled voice,

"How did they – find you?"

Lord Harleston thought that he should have expected her to ask this question sooner or later and he should have had an answer ready.

After a short hesitation he replied,

"Every cowboy, whoever he works for, would know the Altmans."

"It is – very kind of them to take – me in," Nelda murmured.

Lord Harleston felt her search for his hand, which was lying on the outside of the patchwork quilt.

"I am so glad – you were there, because, as you are a member of Papa's family, I don't feel quite so – alone."

He felt her fingers tremble in his as she added,

"But I – am – alone in the world now."

"When you return to England," Lord Harleston replied, "you will find you have a large number of relatives, in fact I often think we have too many."

There was silence.

"Perhaps – they will not like me and – disapprove of Papa."

Lord Harleston sensed that she was going to say 'as you do' and then stopped herself.

"I think once anyone knows you, Nelda," he said rapidly, "they would find, as I have done, that you are brave, self-controlled and very intelligent."

He felt her start in surprise before she asked,

"Do you mean – that? Do you – really mean – it?"

"I promise you I am speaking the truth."

"I am glad – so very – very glad. I know that Papa would want the Head of his Family to like me."

She gave a deep sigh and took her hand away.

"Now I am much – happier," she murmured like a child, "and I will go to – sleep."

She turned on her side and after a little while Lord Harleston could observe by her quiet breathing that she was finally fast asleep.

But he lay awake thinking.

CHAPTER SIX

Lord Harleston opened his eyes and realised that the light in the room came not from the oil lamp, which had gone out, but because the shutters over the window fitted badly.

The yellow lines of sunlight that percolated into the room induced a golden glow and he turned his head to look at Nelda with her head on the pillow beside him.

She looked very lovely, very young and very innocent and, he thought with a twist of his lips, that with his reputation no one, least of all Robert, would believe that he had spent the night beside a beautiful woman without touching her.

He found himself wondering what Nelda would do if he kissed her and decided that she would not be as much shocked as astonished.

He had not missed the fact that she treated him as somebody authoritative and elderly. He might have been her uncle or her father, but in no way as a young man whom she would think of as a suitor.

It was a sobering thought that he appeared so old to somebody so young, but he knew that he had never met anyone like Nelda.

Not that he had ever had anything to do with young girls, but those he had seen occasionally in the houses of his hostesses he had always thought were somewhat gauche and ungainly and certainly painfully shy.

He had expected Nelda to be uncouth and tainted by the life that her father led, but she had surprised him again and again with everything she said and did until he was left completely astounded by her bravery and her self-control.

He knew as she lay there, looking so frail and insubstantial with her eyes closed that it was impossible to imagine any woman of his acquaintance behaving in such an exemplary manner or showing bravery, which was actually more than he would have expected from a man of his own age.

Looking back over what Nelda had experienced in the last five days, he thought that no one would believe it had happened and certainly he himself found it hard to credit that they had both passed unscathed through such traumatic events.

This brought to his attention the fact that the bandage on his arm was uncomfortable and he knew too that he wanted to wash before Nelda was awake.

Carefully, so as not to disturb her, he slipped from the bed and walked silently across the floor on his stockinged feet into the other room.

This also was alight with the sunshine percolating through the shutters and, having closed the bedroom door very softly, he opened first the front door and then pulled back the shutters on the windows so that sunshine and fresh air flooded in.

It was still very early with a faint haze over the Plains, but he was sure that Waldo and his father's servants would soon arrive in search of them.

What was important was that they should not think that he and Nelda had been killed with the rest of the party, so he must keep a watch out for anyone passing the house.

He therefore kept looking out of the window while he washed at the sink using up all the water that remained in the ewer. He had noticed, however, that there was a washstand with a china bowl in the bedroom and made a mental note that he must fetch some more from the well as Nelda would need it.

He was determined that she should not go outside the house until they were rescued in case she discovered the dead Arapaho or the farmer and his wife who had been scalped.

It was all so unpleasant that Lord Harleston muttered to himself,

'The sooner we get away from here the better!'

Then he thought that he was being somewhat ungrateful to Fate, which had provided them with a safe and fairly comfortable place to stay the night in rather than in the open where they might have been intimidated by wild animals and perhaps more Indians roving the Plains.

By the time he had washed and undone the bandage to see that his wound was healing without becoming inflamed he put on his riding boots and felt more presentable.

He was aware that he needed a shave, his cravat, which he had been wearing when the Indian was trying to throttle him, was in a deplorable condition and the sleeve was half-torn from his riding coat.

Nevertheless he and Nelda were alive and that was really the only thing that mattered.

He was just wondering whether he should wake her so that she could be dressed before the search party arrived when, glancing out of the window, he saw, as he had hoped, that in the distance there was a small cavalcade of men.

He snatched up the white cloth that Nelda had washed his wound with and, hurrying out onto the verandah, he stood there waving it.

*

"All I can say is thank God that pretty child had the sense to make you hide among the trees rather than try to join the others," Mr. Altman said fervently.

After they arrived at the Ranch, they had recounted and discussed what had happened until Lord Harleston began to think that there could be nothing more to say.

He was well aware that it was a great shock to Mr. Altman that he had lost his wagons and so many of his servants, while all Mrs. Altman could think of was that her beloved son had escaped because he had ridden on ahead of them.

Waldo, on the other hand, had been ashamed of what he thought of as 'deserting his post'.

"I should have stayed with them," he kept saying.

"What could you or I have done?" Lord Harleston asked. "I think there must have been nearly fifty Indians against sixteen in charge of the wagons. Quite frankly I feel that, even if you and I had been with them, there would have been no chance of our survival."

"I can't understand why the Arapaho are on the warpath at this particular moment," Mr. Altman remarked. "They have indeed always been more rebellious against the white man's encroachment than the Cheyenne, but we have had no trouble for a long time."

"I'm sure it's due to what the Utes are doing on the other side of the Rockies, Pa," Waldo stated.

"You may be right," Mr. Altman conceded, "and I heard yesterday from somebody who was passing through that they have sent in Military aid from Fort Stephen."

"Where is that?" Lord Harleston enquired.

"In Wyoming. It's just over the border where the Northern Utes are attacking farmsteads and carrying away their livestock."

"As they did at the one where we spent last night."

Exactly," Mr. Altman agreed. "You're fortunate, my Lord, not to have been there when the Indians killed the farmer. He was a decent man and I shall now have to try to replace him."

The talk of the tragedy went on and on and Lord Harleston was glad that Mrs. Altman had insisted when they reached the Ranch that Nelda should go to bed and rest. She therefore did not have to listen to the lurid and depressing accounts of what had occurred.

"It seems terrible that a girl of that age should have to pass through such a ghastly ordeal," Mrs. Altman exclaimed to Lord Harleston.

She was a plump, jolly middle-aged woman, who was obviously only too willing to mother Nelda as she mothered her own children.

"She has been extraordinarily brave," Lord Harleston replied.

"She would need to be," Mrs. Altman said, "with first her father and mother being killed in that inhuman manner and then escaping herself by only a hair's breadth."

Lord Harleston had sensed with a perception that was unusual for him that Nelda would not want anybody to know that she had killed a man to save his life.

He had therefore not mentioned it to Waldo when he had arrived at the farm with the rescue team, but had merely told him first that they had stayed there the night and secondly where the men with the wagons had been killed by the Indians.

"I'm thankful you're all right," Waldo said. "When we realised late last night that you'd not arrived and something awful might have happened to you, Pa and Ma were in a real state."

After the arrival of the rescue party at the farm, Lord Harleston had not wished to talk too much about it until Waldo had inspected the wreckage of the wagons and he had suggested that they go there while Nelda dressed to be ready for their return.

Accordingly the rescue party had moved away and, when they had gone, Lord Harleston knocked on the bedroom door.

"I am nearly ready," Nelda had called out.

He waited until a few minutes later she opened the door and he saw that she was dressed.

"I heard voices and recognised Waldo's," she explained.

"They will be coming back for us in a short while."

Nelda came into the living room, looked at the stove and said,

"I am afraid there are no eggs left – but I can make you some tea if you want something to drink."

"I think we might both have a cup of tea," Lord Harleston answered, "and I will draw some water from the well, which I suspect is outside. You see to the fire."

He picked up the ewer and, as he was passing Nelda towards the front door, she said,

"Please – I have something to – ask you, my Lord."

"What is it? " he enquired.

"I-I would rather you did not tell – anybody I – killed the – Indian."

Lord Harleston smiled.

"As it happens, I had already thought that you would want to keep it a secret."

"I could not – bear to talk about it and, if you have to tell Waldo or his men that he is dead – please say that you killed him – yourself."

"I understand exactly what you feel about it, Nelda."

He went outside to find the well and then fill the ewer with water.

As he was doing so, he thought that few women would have had the quickness or the resolution to save his life and if they had done so most would undoubtedly have wished to take all the credit for it.

'She is certainly very different from any woman I have known,' he told himself again.

Then he could not help wondering what sort of life she had lived with her father which could make her ready to tackle any situation however horrifying.

Looking at her as she boiled the kettle and made them both a cup of tea, he thought that she seemed so graceful and fragile that it seemed impossible that she had ever done anything but sit in a ladylike way in a drawing room making polite conversation to elderly visitors.

To think of her coming into contact in any way with the rough types who mined for gold and were dirty, unshaven and uncouth and, Lord Harleston was sure, foul-mouthed, was to stretch the imagination.

'I must hear the rest of her story,' he decided.

Then he told himself that there was plenty of time for him to learn everything he wanted to know before he sent her back to England.

While Nelda was still sleeping or at any rate resting somewhere in the large Ranch, which was much more comfortable and luxurious than Lord Harleston had expected, Waldo took him to see the cattle.

The herds were grazing over some of the two million acres that the Prairie Cattle Company controlled, but Lord Harleston saw only a few hundreds.

He was told about the round-ups and the branding of calves, which took place on a stupendous scale and that each Ranch had a foreman in charge of its cowboys.

Their job was not only to keep track of the cattle but also to round them up to castrate the majority of the young bulls and sear a mark on each calf with the same brand as its mother's.

Lord Harleston found it far more interesting than he had anticipated and he asked many intelligent questions that pleased Mr. Altman. He was amused to hear one of the foremen describe him as 'a regular guy despite the fact he's a 'Limey'.

When he returned to the Ranch in the evening having been in the saddle for nearly six hours, he felt tired, but he had very much enjoyed himself.

"I can quite understand," he said to Mr. Altman, "how fascinating a man could find this sort of life."

"You should try it for yourself some time," Mr. Altman remarked.

"Perhaps I will," Lord Harleston replied, "but first I must return to New York so that I can send Nelda back to England where my family will look after her."

"She's a very pretty young gal," Mr Altman commented, "which is not surprising, seeing how good-looking her father was. I met him a number of times over the years, but I'd no idea he had a wife and daughter."

Lord Harleston remembered Jennie Rogers saying the same thing.

"Surely," he asked, "my cousin must have known some people in the neighbourhood where he was staying besides those he played cards with?"

The contemptuous note was back in his voice, which would have distressed Nelda if she had heard it.

Mr. Altman smiled.

"If 'Handsome Harry', as he was called, mixed with anybody outside of business hours, I never heard of it. Most of the places he lived in had little of what you might call 'social life'."

"So I gather," Lord Harleston nodded.

"I don't mind telling you," Mr. Altman went on confidentially, "it surprised me when Waldo told me who the girl with you was and it was an even bigger surprise when I saw her."

Lord Harleston understood exactly what he was saying without elaborating the point.

Mr. Altman went on, taking time to clarify his thoughts,

"Not that Handsome Harry wasn't a gentleman in his way. In fact, despite the fact that he was too good a player and too lucky at cards to suit most gamblers in this part of the world, they could never accuse him of being anything but straight.'

There was a little pause before Lord Harleston asked,

"Is that true?"

He had always suspected that Harry, when he was desperate for money, cheated in some way or another, which accounted for his being described as being 'swift of hand'.

"Yes, it's true," Mr. Altman said, "and I can assure you, my Lord, that, if a man cheats at cards or anything else in any of our gaming Clubs, he doesn't live for very long!"

Lord Harleston was relieved to know that his worst fears were groundless and it also made it easier to understand Nelda's admiration as well as her love for her father.

'Perhaps I have misjudged Harry,' he thought to himself.

Even so the idea of his dragging his wife and daughter round the mining towns like Silverton and Leadville still made him feel disgusted.

Back at the Ranch Lord Harleston was able to have a good long bath and change into evening clothes before it was time for dinner.

The Altmans dined early as he knew was customary in Colorado, but after a long day's riding, although they had stopped for a sandwich luncheon, Lord Harleston had the appetite of a man who had earned it.

He went down to dinner expectantly to find that there was not only an enormous meal waiting for him but also Nelda.

She was in the low-ceiling sitting room, which had been elaborately built of tree trunks and had a huge open fireplace that could burn a gigantic log.

She was looking exceedingly pretty in a gown that she had borrowed from Waldo's sister, Mattie.

Although Mattie was a pleasant fresh-faced girl, her looks could in no way be compared to Nelda's, but she had a slim elegant figure thanks to the amount of riding she did.

Her gowns therefore fitted Nelda as if they had been made for her.

The one she was wearing this evening was a young girl's dress and very becoming. The soft pink of the material trimmed with white lace seemed to throw into prominence the whiteness of her skin and the pale gold of her hair.

Lord Harleston thought, although he was not quite sure, that her eyes lit up when she saw him and he crossed the room to her side to say,

"How are you, Nelda? Did you sleep well?"

"I feel rather like Rip Van Winkle, but now I am awake I am upset that – I missed riding with you."

"It was a long day," Lord Harleston replied, "which would have been far too much for you, but I am sure that Waldo is only too willing to tell you all about it."

"I've something better to talk about than cattle," Waldo exclaimed and Lord Harleston laughed.

It was obvious long before dinner was finished that Waldo had a great deal to say to Nelda and he was clearly already infatuated with her.

Lord Harleston saw his mother looking at him speculatively several times and wondered what the Altmans would think if their son asked Nelda to marry him and she accepted.

Then he frowned at the idea and told himself that Nelda was far too young, although he had actually not asked her age, to even think of marriage.

He thought once again that the sooner he heard the whole of her life's history the better.

However there was no chance that evening for them to talk without being overheard and anyway she was being monopolised by Waldo.

The next morning Lord Harleston found that he was expected to view more cattle and he and Waldo left the house before any of the womenfolk were awake.

Fortunately they made it a short expedition and were back at the Ranch in time for luncheon.

It was then that Lord Harleston said firmly that they must leave for Denver the next day.

As he spoke, he saw an expression on Nelda's face that he could not quite interpret and he did not know whether she was glad to be leaving or whether she would rather have stayed longer with the Altmans.

Whatever her feelings, Lord Harleston was determined that he would take her to New York as quickly as possible and in case he had other ideas he knew it was important that he should talk to her alone.

Accordingly when the meal was finished and everybody moved into the sitting room where there were comfortable armchairs, Lord Harleston said to Mrs. Altman,

"I would like if possible to have a word alone with Nelda. Is there another room where we could talk? "

"Of course," Mrs. Altman replied. "There is what we call the 'writing room', although it is seldom used."

She led the way as she spoke down a passage, opened a door into what was a much smaller but attractive sitting room again built with wooden walls and containing a large fireplace.

There was a long desk in front of one of the windows, but what caught Nelda's eye immediately was a large bookcase filled with leather-bound volumes.

Once again Lord Harleston suspected that, like those in the Altman house in Denver, they had been bought for their decorative qualities.

The moment Mrs. Altman left them alone Nelda went to the bookcase to gaze at the books with the same expression in her eyes, Lord Harleston thought with amusement, that he had seen on the faces of other women he had known when staring in the window of a jeweller's shop.

"Books!" she exclaimed excitedly, "The difficulty is going to be to decide which one I will have time to read before we have to leave."

"Before you choose one I want to talk to you, Nelda."

She took her eyes from the books reluctantly and moved towards him as he seated himself in a big leather-covered chair.

He waited until she too had sat down before he began,

"Before I can make any plans for your future I have to ask you some quite simple questions which, until I know the answers, may seem strange."

Nelda looked at him tentatively and he thought not only how lovely she was but also that if he had never met her before he would have found her very intelligent and, although it seemed impossible, very well educated.

Because it was the last thought that came to his mind, he said,

"You told me that you could read French. What I have been wondering is how, in this strange life you have led with your father, you have managed to have an education of any sort."

Nelda smiled.

"I suppose that might sound odd to somebody coming from England, but, because Mama herself had a better education than most of her contemporaries, she was determined that I should not miss having the sort of Governesses whom she had when she was my age."

Lord Harleston waited and a little shyly she went on,

"Sometimes it was very difficult, but, of course, Mama taught me herself and wherever we went she was clever enough to find University teachers who were grateful to be able to earn a little extra money."

Still Lord Harleston did not speak and Nelda went on quickly,

"I know what you are thinking and, of course, there were times when we could not afford to pay anybody, but Mama insisted that I went on with my lessons, finding books for me to study and making me sit examinations which she set for me. And naturally we searched and searched for books and more books."

The way she spoke told Lord Harleston that this had been an excitement in itself, rather like a treasure hunt, and when Nelda and her mother did find a book on any particular subject, unlike other children, she would read it avidly because it had been so precious for her.

"That is certainly surprising," he said aloud, "and I suppose first I should have asked you how old you are."

"I am nearly nineteen."

Lord Harleston looked at her as if he could not believe what he had just heard.

"I thought you were much younger than nineteen!" he exclaimed.

Nelda laughed.

"Papa has always said how young I looked and he could not believe that I was born so many years ago. But of one thing I am certain about, I shall grow older!"

Lord Harleston laughed too.

"That is indisputable and now tell me more about your life."

Nelda gave a little sigh.

"I suppose, as Mama has always said, it was a very strange one and, when I told you I had never had a friend, it was true."

"It sounds extraordinary, but why?" Lord Harleston enquired.

"Because Papa would never let us mix with the people in the towns where we lived and, even when we were in places like San Francisco or St. Louis, Mama and I met no one."

Lord Harleston stared at her.

"How is that possible? I don't understand."

Nelda looked down and her lashes were dark against her pale cheeks before she replied,

"I know you did not approve of Papa and the way he made – money by playing cards – but then he did not – approve of – himself."

There was a little silence.

Then Lord Harleston commented,

"I still don't think I understand."

"Papa always told us how wild he was as a young man," Nelda said after a moment, "and how many escapades he became involved in. But, when he met Mama, everything changed."

"Where did they get married? "

"They were married before they went aboard the ship that carried them across the Atlantic."

Lord Harleston realised that this was something his relatives did not know, but he did not interrupt and Nelda went on,

"Papa loved Mama with all his heart and he always told her that he wanted to give her everything in the world because she had given up so much for him. But the only way he could make any money at all was by playing cards."

"And you say that he was ashamed of it?" Lord Harleston questioned.

"Not perhaps at first because, when they were in New York, Papa got to know some nice people. But then he found that he was too good a player for what he called 'social games' and he joined what was known as 'The Big Boys'."

"I know what you mean,"

"It was after I was born that Papa began to grow bored or else he was too good for the people he was playing with. Therefore we moved on, going from one town to another, until the gamblers claimed that Papa was too good and so we had to move on again."

"That seems an extraordinary compliment," Lord Harleston said pausing to find the right words.

"Papa said once that somebody had told him that a card player of his ability was one in a million."

"I am sure that is true."

"But you will understand, since Papa had no money, except what he made, that, as soon as men began to turn away from him because he had won too much, he had to find 'pastures new'."

"Yes, I see,' but you were telling me what happened to you and your mother."

"I suppose quite frankly that Papa did not think the men he played with were good enough for us to know and so we never met anybody or went anywhere, except with him when he was not in the gaming rooms."

"I have never heard anything so amazing!" Lord Harleston exclaimed. "It must have been a very dull life."

Nelda smiled and shook her head.

"Only if you look at it from a social point of view. Intellectually Mama and I had a wonderful time. When we could afford it, we went to concerts, theatres and the Opera, we visited Museums if there were any and, of course, all the time we were on the lookout for books."

"And do you mean to say," Lord Harleston asked, "that you had no friends of your own age?"

"I did not want any," Nelda replied, "since both Mama and Papa were to me the most fascinating people in the whole world."

"And yet though never meeting people in what you might call your 'own class'," Lord Harleston said after a moment, "you were still allowed to tend the wounds of miners and outcasts, which I should have thought was certainly something that your father would not have permitted."

"He would have forbidden it if he could," Nelda admitted, "but Mama said that suffering was something that she could not ignore and pass by on the other side. When she was really determined to help somebody who was in pain, no one, not even Papa, could stop her."

"That you should have lived such a life is the most astounding story I have ever heard of!" Lord Harleston said.

"I was sure you would think like that," Nelda answered. "At the same time I do want you to understand that Papa was doing what he thought was best for me and, whatever you may have thought about him, you certainly could not disapprove of Mama."

"No, of course not," Lord Harleston agreed.

He did not miss what was almost a challenging note in Nelda's voice and he went on,

"Now you have explained all this to me, I can tell you truthfully that I do *not* now disapprove of your father as I did before and I understand that, as there was no other way for him to earn money, he had to gamble."

"I think he enjoyed it most of the time, although sometimes when things went wrong, he would say, 'I wish to God I need never see another card again! I ought to have done what my father wanted and become a Parson'!"

She smiled before she continued,

"Then Mama and I would laugh and we would tease him and say that the Church would be full of women who admired him and would be thinking of him rather than saying their prayers."

Lord Harleston chuckled.

"I am sure that is true. I remember thinking when I was a small boy that your father was the most handsome man I had ever seen in my life."

"Mama was very beautiful too and wherever we went people used to stare at them as if they could not believe their eyes."

"Yes, and I can see the resemblance in you. But there is a very different sort of life waiting for you in England."

He paused before he went on to say,

"You looked so young when I first saw you that I was planning to send you to a school, but I know now that is quite unnecessary. Instead I will send you to my relatives and you will become a *debutante*. They will introduce you to Society and, of course, you will attend a 'Drawing Room' at Buckingham Palace and make your curtsey to Queen Victoria – "

He was thinking aloud and seeing mentally his plans ahead of him.

Then Nelda made a little sound, which he realised to his surprise was one of protest.

He stopped speaking and Nelda came in quickly,

"Please – please – I don't want to be a – *debutante*!"

"Why not? "

"Because I would feel frightened and out of place."

"Then what do you want?" Lord Harleston asked her sharply.

There was a long pause before Nelda responded in a very small voice,

"P-please – could I not – stay with – you?"

Lord Harleston stared at her as if he could not have heard her aright.

Then he replied,

"You must see that that is impossible."

"Why?"

He smiled before he said cynically,

"For one reason, because I am too young, although you may not think it, to look after a young girl and secondly because it would bore me to distraction to have to attend the sort of balls you would go to."

"I don't wish to – go to balls. I want to study – I want to ride – and I would be happy in the country – in the house where you live – and which Papa has so often described to me."

"It's impossible, Nelda."

He rose from the chair where he was sitting and walked to the window.

He was wondering how he could explain that, if he kept Nelda with him, his reputation, which in a different way was not unlike her father's, would ensure that a very different interpretation would be put on their relationship.

He stood staring out on the sunlit Prairie without really seeing it.

Then he started as, without hearing her move, Nelda had come to his side.

"Please – please," she implored him, "let me be with you. I don't want to be with a lot of – strange people who – if they are relations of either Papa or Mama will – not have me because I am their daughter – just as you – hated me at first."

Lord Harleston drew in his breath.

"Because you are very different from what I expected, I promise to see to it that no one in England will hate you and, because you are a Harle, the family will welcome you and want to be kind to you."

Even as he spoke he knew that this was not quite true.

The Harles would be curious about Nelda because she was Handsome Harry's daughter, but neither they nor the Marlowes would ever forget or really forgive the way that they had eloped.

Also, as he well knew himself, the story of Harry's gambling life in America had lost nothing in the telling.

While he was thinking, Nelda had drawn a little nearer to him and now she put her hand on his arm to say,

"Yesterday you said I was brave – but really I am a – coward. I am afraid – of going to England – afraid of meeting my – relations and most of all afraid of – leaving you."

Because Lord Harleston was a very intelligent man, he understood exactly what she was feeling or perhaps it was because his intuition told him more than what Nelda was saying in actual words.

It was understandable that now that she was alone she would be afraid of other people, especially those who would criticise her father.

Lord Harleston could see her defiantly fighting a losing battle to defend him and he was suddenly aware how vulnerable she was and, despite her book learning, completely ignorant of people.

Of course she would have a difficult time with her relations, whether they were Harles or Marlowes.

What would make it even more difficult was the certainty that the women would be jealous of her beauty and the men, knowing of Harry's wild reputation before his alleged reformation, would approach her without the respect that she would be entitled to in other circumstances.

'What am I to do with her?' Lord Harleston asked himself.

Then an answer came to his mind that he did not want to hear.

*

At dinner that evening Waldo was so ardent in his attentions towards Nelda that Lord Harleston was aware that she was becoming nervous and even seemed to be shrinking away as if he encroached on her.

As he watched her across the table, he found that he could read her thoughts and sense her feelings.

He knew that in the future this was something that would happen over and over again with almost every man she met and she would not be able to deal with them on her own.

Now he noticed, even though he appeared to be talking to his hostess, that she kept glancing at him as if for support and he had the feeling that she reassured herself that nothing could harm her because he was there.

'It's a mistake to allow her to come to rely on me like this,' he deduced.

Then he knew that, because of the strange unbelievably lonely life that she had led before she had lost her mother and father, there was no one else.

Everything that for her had meant stability had gone and now she could only cling to him as a drowning man would cling to a spar of wood in a tempestuous sea.

'I shall have to do something about her,' he decided, but he had no idea what that could possibly be.

When dinner was finished and the servants had cleared away the plates, Mrs. Altman said,

"It does seem a pity, Lord Harleston, that you have to leave us so soon. I know you are thinking of sending Nelda back to England, but I was wondering if she would not be happier in America and, if so, she could live with us. She would be a nice companion to Mattie and the two girls could have fun together."

It sounded, Lord Harleston reflected, an excellent idea on the surface.

But even as he began to thank Mrs. Altman for suggesting it, he saw the terror in Nelda's eyes and knew that she could not bear that he should leave her with the Altmans, pleasant though they were.

When he went to bed without having the chance of an intimate word again with Nelda, he found himself unable to sleep.

He lay awake thinking over what a problem she had become and how quite unexpectedly her difficulties seemed to fill his mind to the exclusion of his own.

'One thing is certain she cannot wander about with me in America,' he reasoned.

Then he was astonished that he should even contemplate such an idea. What could he do with a young girl who he had no interests in common with?

Yet he was aware that Nelda was not only unlike any young girl he could imagine, she was also unlike any woman he had ever come across.

Looking back he knew that one of the reasons why he became bored so quickly with the women he made love to was that he always knew in advance what they would say and do at any particular moment.

He could anticipate their answer to every question he put to them and he could never talk to them in the same way that he could talk to Robert or any of his other men friends.

Now he had the idea that he could have a great deal to discuss with Nelda and that her knowledge equalled and in some cases exceeded his own.

Whenever she managed to avoid the whispered conversation that Waldo was trying to have with her, he noticed that she talked intelligently and knowledgeably with Mr. Altman about the rearing of cattle.

She also discussed the discoveries of gold and silver deposits in the mountains and, more surprisingly, the political situation in America compared with other parts of the world.

Lord Harleston had already learnt that Mr. Altman was anxious on his retirement to run for Congress and, once launched on his favourite subject, he could be very verbose about the leadership coming from the White House.

Lord Harleston was out of his depth in such topics, for he had never studied American Politics in any detail.

But Nelda knew not only how to say exactly the right thing to stimulate Mr. Altman in the defence of his policies but also to confound him on several points in a manner that made him laugh.

He said at length that if she went on like this she would find herself being elected as the first woman to Congress.

'She is very clever in more ways than one,' Lord Harleston admitted to himself.

But that made his problem more difficult rather than easier.

He knew that, if she had been a stupid cow-like type of girl, she would have accepted the suggestion that Mrs. Altman had made for her gratefully and without prevaricating.

As it was, he was quite certain that she would fight him in every possible way to avoid being sent like an unwanted parcel back to England.

Tossing and turning as the night went on, Lord Harleston found himself asking over and over again,

'What shall I do? What *can* I do?'

Then he saw, as clearly as if she was lying beside him, Nelda asleep with her eyelashes dark against her cheeks and her perfectly curved lips just parted as if they waited for him to kiss them.

CHAPTER SEVEN

Lord Harleston was dressing and at the same time instructing one of Mr. Altman's servants how to pack his clothes.

He was missing Portman more than he liked to admit and he thought that, when he reached New York, he would try to find an English valet to replace him.

Certainly the American who was helping him now was of little or no use.

Fortunately Portman had not unpacked most of the trunks and the only things to add to them were the clothes that Lord Harleston had used before leaving for the Ranch.

He was just fastening a cufflink when there came a knock on the door and, without waiting for a reply, Waldo opened it and put his head in to say,

"Can I speak to you for a moment, my Lord?"

"Yes, of course," Lord Harleston replied.

"You've plenty of time," Waldo informed him, "and Pa's making arrangements to have the Company coach attached to the train."

"That is very kind of him."

Lord Harleston knew that he would much rather travel as he usually did in England in a private coach than in the rather cramped, so-called 'drawing rooms' that were the best that any passenger could book.

Waldo, however, was not listening. He made a gesture to the servant that they wanted to be alone and the man left the room.

Then he turned to Lord Harleston,

"I want to talk to you."

"What about, Waldo?"

"Nelda."

Lord Harleston braced himself.

He anticipated what Waldo was going to say and was wondering how he should reply.

The young man was obviously slightly embarrassed and moved restlessly about the bedroom until he finally announced,

"I want to marry her!"

Lord Harleston's eyes were on his cufflinks as he replied slowly,

"I thought that might be in your mind."

"She's the most beautiful adorable girl I've ever seen in my life!" Waldo enthused. "In fact I've never known anyone like her."

Lord Harleston thought that he might truthfully say the same. Instead he waited and Waldo went on,

"I'd like to persuade you to stay here longer, but if you're determined to go to New York, then I'd like to follow you tomorrow or the next day."

Lord Harleston turned from the dressing table to look at the young man.

He was certainly good-looking and had a frank open manner that he had liked from his first acquaintance. But to Lord Harleston he seemed very young and in some ways immature.

At the same time Nelda was young too.

He wondered if perhaps such a marriage might be a successful one. It would certainly solve his own personal problem regarding her.

Then realising that Waldo was waiting apprehensively for his answer, he asked,

"Have you spoken to Nelda about this?"

"I tried to last night," he replied, "but she was very evasive and, I think, shy."

Lord Harleston thought that he would replace the word 'shy' by 'afraid'.

He had seen the look in Nelda's eyes when Waldo was talking to her and he was quite sure that, because of the extraordinary way that she had been brought up, she had never had any contact with a man who might be falling in love with her.

With him she was completely unselfconscious, but Lord Harleston was well aware that she thought of him really as her only rock of safety and security in her loneliness and he could understand that Waldo's impulsive approach would scare her.

Aloud he said,

"Nelda is very young and I have learnt how her father insisted on keeping her away from the people he associated with. As she therefore has had no friends, I think it will be some time before she can adjust herself to the idea of marriage."

"That's why I'd like her to stay here and get used to me," Waldo replied, "but it might be rather difficult."

The way he spoke made Lord Harleston ask,

"What do you mean by that?"

He thought for a moment that Waldo was not going to answer him until, after a distinct hesitation, he said,

"I don't think my father and mother would exactly encourage the idea."

Lord Harleston was surprised.

He thought, because Mrs. Altman seemed so kind and maternal towards Nelda and Mr. Altman was obviously very sorry for the tragedy that she had encountered, that they were genuinely fond of her.

"You have discussed this with them?" he asked.

"Yes, I mentioned it after Nelda had gone to bed last night."

Lord Harleston remembered that he too had retired early and so Waldo had been able to talk to his family alone.

"I would be interested to hear what your father said."

Again Waldo seemed to hesitate.

Then after a long moment he replied,

"I think perhaps I'd better be frank with you and say that my father's not at all keen that I should marry Handsome Harry's daughter."

Lord Harleston stiffened.

Although he was aware that this was a reaction that he might have expected from Mr. Altman, he was so proud of his family that it seemed incredible that anybody in this country would not be glad to be connected with the Harles.

"He did say," Waldo went on, "that Nelda was the prettiest girl he had ever seen and that he liked her, but he didn't think that socially she would be accepted in Denver."

Lord Harleston was completely taken by surprise.

He had thought of Denver as basically a mining town although he had read about the Society that had grown up there and had seen the enormous and grand town houses that were being built.

But it had never struck him that, just as in England and in other countries in Europe, in Denver there were already both upper and lower strata of social life and the upper would be very particular as to whom they admitted into their circle.

As if Waldo knew what he was thinking, he said,

"Some of the newcomers, even though they're as rich as Croesus, are more or less ostracised. They've done everything they can to be accepted, but they're still left on the outside."

"What you are saying," Lord Harleston remarked slowly, "is that your father does not think that Nelda Harle is good enough for you."

He could not help sounding sarcastic, but Waldo did not seem to notice.

He only walked to the window to say,

"Aw, Pa'll come round eventually. What he's fussing about at the moment is keeping a low profile for when he runs for Congress."

"I should have thought, considering how much she seems to know about American Politics, that Nelda would be seen as an asset," Lord Harleston remarked.

He did not know why he was defending Nelda so aggressively, but it irritated him to learn that Mr. Altman did not think her good enough for his son.

Waldo did not reply and after a moment Lord Harleston asked,

"What did your mother say?"

"I'd rather not tell you that," Waldo answered after a pause.

"If we are being frank with each other," Lord Harleston said, "and, as Nelda's Guardian, I would prefer to know the truth."

Waldo shuffled his feet and with his hands deep in his pockets he looked uncomfortable.

"You're not going to like this," he said at length.

"I am still prepared to listen to it," Lord Harleston replied.

"Ma's old fashioned, so you can't really blame her," he said even more uncomfortably, "but she thought, as you'd more or less compromised Nelda's reputation by staying the night alone with her in a farmhouse, that if anybody should marry her it ought to be you!"

If he had fired a pistol at him, Lord Harleston could not have been more astounded.

Because it had been such an obvious solution indeed the only possible one after their terrifying drama of escaping from the Indians, it had never struck him for one moment that anybody could think it wrong that he and Nelda had taken refuge under the same roof for one night.

Of course, if Mrs. Altman had known that they had slept in the same bed, he could have better understood her attitude.

But there had been nothing he could do but stay with Nelda in the farmhouse, although he supposed it was indeed from her point of view a compromising situation.

Because he was startled, he replied angrily,

"I have never heard such utter rubbish in all my life! Nelda and I had just escaped death and there was even an Indian lurking in the house when we reached it. In the circumstances we could think of nothing except to thank God that we were still alive."

"I understand, of course, I understand," Waldo said soothingly. "But you know what women are like. Actually I don't think it was Ma's idea, but the servants have talked about how pretty Nelda is and you being a Lord and all that sort of thing."

"Gossip! Gossip!" Lord Harleston asserted contemptuously. "One thing I really dislike is gossiping women who have nothing else to do but defame their own sex."

Even as he spoke he remembered that the reason why the Prince of Wales had informed him that he should marry Dolly was that he was supposed to have damaged her reputation.

There was some justification for the Prince of Wales believing it, he thought, but where Nelda was concerned it was totally different.

He picked up his coat from the chair and put it on in such a manner that it might have been a coat of mail and he was preparing to go into battle.

"I didn't want to upset you," Waldo muttered, "but you did tell me you wanted to hear what Pa and Ma had said."

"Yes, I did," Lord Harleston conceded, "and I suppose it is what I might have expected, although it had never struck me that anybody would think such things least of all about Nelda."

"They're not thinking of Nelda," Waldo replied, "but of me!"

This was obvious and Lord Harleston thought that he had been needlessly aggressive.

~157~

"What I'm asking you," Waldo continued, "is how I can see Nelda again. How long do you intend to stay in New York?"

"I have not yet made up my mind," Lord Harleston replied. "As you are well aware, the first thing we have to do it to buy some clothes for her and I am most grateful to your sister for providing her with something to wear until I am able to do so."

"That should take some time at any rate," Waldo calculated, "and, if I do join you, will you allow me to see as much of her as is possible?"

It was the sort of question that Lord Harleston felt reluctant to answer and, playing for time, he replied,

"I think, before I make any promises or arrangements on Nelda's behalf, I should first discuss it with her. It must be up to her whether she wishes to see you again and let me make it quite clear that, as her Guardian, I would never press her into marriage with anybody unless she was willing and in love."

"I'll *make* her love me," Waldo contended. "Of course she is your responsibility now that her father and mother are dead, but she's always lived in America and I can't believe that she really wants to go back to England."

"All the same she is English."

"Yes, of course, but I bet she feels that she belongs here."

Waldo spoke optimistically and Lord Harleston then had the idea that he was trying to persuade himself that Nelda would be ready to marry him, even though he suspected that her feelings were very different.

He walked towards the door ready to go downstairs for breakfast, but Waldo was looking out of the window and said,

"I've met a lot of girls in one way or another, but I've never felt like this about any of them."

"You are still very young and it is a mistake to get married too quickly."

"It's not a mistake when you're absolutely sure that you've met the right person," Waldo replied, "and what I'm asking, my Lord, is will you help me?"

"As I have already said, it is entirely up to Nelda."

Waldo made a helpless gesture with his hands.

"I suppose that's the best you can do and I must just hope when I come to New York that Nelda'll be more encouraging than she is at the moment."

Lord Harleston felt that there was nothing more he could do and pulled open the door, saying,

"I understand from your father that he is sending a large escort with us."

"Twenty men who are known as the best shots on the Prairie," Waldo confirmed.

Lord Harleston instinctively put his hand to his pocket to see if his pistol was there. That would make twenty-one and in England he was considered an outstanding game shot.

Now that Waldo had told him of his feelings for Nelda and his father's and mother's reaction, he thought that there was a slight reserve about Mr. and Mrs. Altman that had not been there before and he sensed that they were relieved that he and Nelda were leaving.

Because she was looking so exquisitely pretty in a travelling gown and cloak owned by Mattie with a very *chic* little bonnet trimmed with flowers, he could sympathise with Waldo.

There was no doubt that the young man was looking miserable and, although his father said that he had work for him to do on the Ranch, he insisted that he should accompany them to Denver.

"I can't see any point in your going there just for one night," Mrs. Altman said sharply.

"Aw, don't fuss, Ma," Waldo answered. " I'll be all right."

Mrs. Altman pressed her lips together as if afraid that she might say too much and she would be sorry for it.

Lord Harleston thought it was not only that she was upset at Waldo's feelings for Nelda but that any mother would worry about her son travelling into possible danger.

Despite the escort there was always the chance that the Indians would attack them again.

*

However the long journey was accomplished much more quickly than the journey out to the Ranch, because they had no wagons with them and the trip was completely uneventful.

There was no sign of any Indians and the Plains looked lovely in the sunshine while the first sight of the Rockies with their snow-capped peaks made Lord Harleston think that it was one of the most beautiful places he had ever seen in all his travels.

They entered Denver and there were the great mansions with their conglomeration of styles and the streets filled with traffic as they drove towards the Railway Station.

It was growing late and the sun was now low on the horizon as they waited at the Station for the long train with its huge engine to come slowly into the platform.

During the ten years since the Denver Pacific had first puffed into Union Station, new railroads had been laid over all Colorado spanning the deep canyons, high passes and precipitous cliffs.

To Lord Harleston's surprise the Prairie Cattle Company's private coach compared favourably with the private trains and coaches that he travelled on in England.

There was a large bedroom and two small ones, a drawing room with comfortable chairs and a servant to travel with them to serve their meals.

Also, as Waldo pointed out proudly, there was a private bar, which supplied every drink a traveller could possibly need.

Because it was obvious to Lord Harleston how very much in love Waldo was with Nelda, he thought it was only fair to give him a chance to say 'goodbye' to her without being overheard.

He therefore deliberately left them in the drawing room and walked to the door of the coach to stand gazing at the commotion on the platform.

There were passengers struggling to find their seats, frightened dogs muzzled and on leads and a great amount of luggage, mailbags and other packages being bundled into the Guard's Van.

He had only stood there for a minute when Nelda joined him.

"People always seem to be so – agitated when they are on the Station platforms," she said in a strange little voice. "Papa used to say he thought it was because they are – afraid of trains."

Without looking at her Lord Harleston knew that she was frightened and he turned from the door and walked back into the drawing room.

Waldo was there with a scowl on his face and Lord Harleston realised that, whatever he had said to Nelda, she had certainly not responded favourably.

"Goodbye, Waldo," he said, "and thank you for entertaining me so well. When you see Jennie Rogers, give her my best regards."

Waldo grinned.

"I will certainly do so and I bet she's sorry not to have seen you again, my Lord."

"Tell her I shall be looking forward to renewing my acquaintance with her the next time I come to Denver."

Lord Harleston was just speaking casually, but he knew by the expression in his eyes that Waldo thought he was implying that Nelda would eventually marry him. In that case, if he came back to Denver, it would be to visit her.

Waldo put out his hand to Nelda.

"Goodbye, Nelda," he sighed. "Remember what I said to you."

She did not look at him, but replied in a low voice,

"I will – remember."

"Well, take care of yourself."

He looked at her for a long moment and then impulsively he put out his hands, held her by the shoulders and kissed her first on one cheek and then on the other.

"I love you!" he murmured. "Don't you forget it!"

Then, as the Guard's whistle shrilled, he swung himself down from the coach onto the platform.

The train began to move and Waldo ran beside the carriage. Lord Harleston was aware that it was with an effort that Nelda went to the window to wave her hand.

He waved too until with much puffing and clouds of smoke they had left Denver Station behind and their last sight of Waldo.

Because the train was swaying uncomfortably, Lord Harleston sat down hurriedly in one of the armchairs.

"I should take off your bonnet and make yourself comfortable," he said to Nelda, "we have a long journey in front of us."

"Yes – of course," she agreed.

She walked towards the other half of the coach and Lord Harleston could hear her speaking to the servant who was carrying into the bedrooms the luggage that they would require on the journey.

It was only later he was to discover that she had taken one of the small bedrooms for herself and leaving him the large one.

But for the moment he was thinking that, as he had watched Waldo kiss Nelda, he had experienced a very strange sensation that was different from any feeling he had ever known before.

It had been so surprising that for a moment he had felt that it could not be real.

Yet now he knew that his first instinct had been to knock the young man down because he was touching Nelda, but his second was an emotion that he had never experienced before, which he was honest enough to admit was *jealousy*.

He could hardly believe it and hardly credit that he was not just imagining what he felt or that the long drive from the Ranch had affected him mentally.

Now sitting alone as the train gathered speed, he was forced to admit to himself that what he felt for Nelda was different and yet in some ways very familiar.

It seemed to him incredible, utterly and completely incredible, that, when she had stood at the window watching the Denver platform and Waldo fade out of sight, he had felt his heart pounding in a very odd way and the blood throbbing in his temples.

He wanted at that moment to put his arms round Nelda, hold her close to him and tell her not to be afraid and he would protect her against Waldo and any other men who approached her.

In fact he would prevent them from doing so.

He thought for one second that he was thinking of her and then realised that actually he had been thinking about himself.

'It cannot be true,' he muttered beneath his breath.

How could this girl, whom he had bought for hard cash even while he despised and disliked the whole idea of her, have suddenly become a very desirable woman instead of the encumbrance who he had been convinced would be a confounded nuisance.

That was what he had felt until she had cried tempestuously against his shoulder after the Indian war cries had faded into silence.

Then he had wanted to comfort, protect and fight for her.

He remembered the silkiness of her hair and the way that, with a courage he admired more than he could possibly say, she had forced away her tears and set off bravely to walk hand-in-hand with him to find somewhere where they could shelter for the night.

Then, with a bravery that had again astounded him, she had saved his life.

Even then, although it must have been terrifying, she had not cried or been hysterical, and only later, when her fear had been too agonising to suffer alone, she had come to him for help.

When he had lain by her side in the darkness of the shuttered room, he had not been aware that what he was feeling when she slipped her hand into his had been *love*.

Because it was so different he had not recognised that the feeling of protection and admiration, which had kept him awake while she slept peacefully like a child beside him, had been love in a very different sense from what he had ever known in his life.

'How could I have guessed, how could I have even imagined that I should love a woman who is so ignorant of the life I have always lived that I shall have to explain it to her as if I was teaching a small child to read and write?' he asked himself.

Then, as he heard Nelda's soft voice in the distance, he not only knew that to teach her about his life at Harleston

Park and in London would be intriguing, but he could also imagine nothing more thrilling or more exciting than to teach her to love him.

As he thought about it, he remembered that Waldo had said the same.

"*I will teach her to love me,*" the young man had said.

Almost like a physical pain in his heart Lord Harleston wondered, if instead of loving him, Nelda would be apprehensive because he had changed from the protective Guardian who had taken the place of her father into a man who wished to be her lover.

Of all the other women he had ever known, and there had been a great number of them, Lord Harleston had never for one moment suspected that a woman he fancied would not respond to his advances.

In fact he knew that usually it was she who made it clear from the very beginning that she desired him and in innumerable cases he was the one who did not respond and who would turn away from a very obvious and unmistakable invitation.

'Supposing Nelda turns away?' Lord Harleston asked himself now.

Never before had he felt so uncertain and so unsure of himself.

Because he was experienced with women and with regard to Nelda especially perceptive and intuitive, he knew when she came back to the drawing room that she was nervous and still upset by Waldo.

She sat down opposite him at a small table and instantly a servant began to bring in the dinner that had been provided for them by Mrs. Altman.

There were tender steaks, which were well cooked, but Lord Harleston was not very hungry.

Every time he looked across the table at Nelda he felt his heart pounding in his chest and it was with the greatest difficulty that he did not try to woo her with the words that he would have used to any other woman in the same circumstances.

Instead he watched her closely.

He realised that she was gradually relaxing and the fear she had felt before they left the Station was giving way to a wide-eyed appreciation of being alone with him and listening to what he had to say.

They talked while they were eating about the kindness of the Altmans, but it was not until the table had been cleared and the only thing left was a glass of French brandy in Lord Harleston's hands that Nelda said,

"It is exciting to be going to New York with you. I feel that we are setting off on an – adventure."

"That is what I thought too," Lord Harleston replied, "and, if it is exciting for you, Nelda, it is equally exciting for me."

She looked at him questioningly before she asked,

"You are – sure of that? I thought perhaps – if I had not been with you – you would have wanted to stay and view the mountains and the mines."

"I would rather be with you," Lord Harleston said quietly and saw what he thought was a light come into her eyes.

Then she asked, and he recognised by the way she asked it, that it was a question that was worrying her,

"How long can we – stay in – New York?"

"For quite a long time. You have not forgotten that I will have to buy you a whole new wardrobe of clothes."

The way that Nelda drew in her breath told him that this was the answer she wanted and she had been afraid that he would send her off to England immediately.

"Until you have done all your shopping," he said, "I think it wisest not to be in touch with any friends I have in the City."

It was an explanation he had kept for Nelda, but actually he was thinking, like Mrs. Altman, that if it was known that he was staying alone with her, it might be disastrous for her reputation.

He had thought, after what Waldo had told him, that he would have to throw himself on the hospitality of the Vanderbilts.

Then, when he was saying 'goodbye', Mr. Altman had solved the problem for him.

"I thought, my Lord," he said, "you wouldn't wish to go to a hotel with Nelda and I've therefore arranged for the apartment that is kept for me and the Directors of the Prairie Cattle Company to be put at your disposal."

"That is extremely kind of you," Lord Harleston exclaimed.

"You'll find it comfortable and there are servants who'll be there to look after you," Mr. Altman went on. "So stay there for as long as you wish."

Lord Harleston could only thank Mr. Altman again.

At the time he thought that this was a Godsend from his own point of view, because he had no wish to involve either Nelda or himself in any gossip that could easily percolate back to England.

Now he knew that he was glad for a very different reason, he would have her to himself.

He was well aware that if they went to the Vanderbilts, Mrs. Alva would immediately involve them in one social gathering after another. Dinner parties, dances and balls would be given in their honour so that it would be almost impossible for him ever to be with Nelda.

'I want her alone,' he whispered to himself.

He just knew, as he looked at her across the table, that surprisingly, in fact astonishingly, when he had least expected it, he had found the woman he wanted to be his wife.

When Nelda had gone to bed, he had sat for a long time in the drawing room thinking about her.

He thought too that no one except perhaps Robert would understand how she was everything he had wanted in his wife and yet at first he had not known it himself.

That his wife would be beautiful went without saying, but what in his dashing raffish career he had never envisaged was that the woman he married would be pure, innocent and untouched.

He was so used to fiery love affairs with women who, because they had lost their hearts as well as their heads where he was concerned, always sighed as they said to him,

"If only we could be married, Selby, it would be a perfect marriage and I would never allow you to look at another woman."

When they had said this, Lord Harleston had always thought a little cynically that it was doubtful if any one woman would satisfy him and that however many good resolutions he made he would find himself after marriage looking round for new amusements and certainly other women.

But almost as if a voice told him so, he knew that with Nelda his marriage would be very different from those that he was familiar with in the Marlborough House Set.

There would be no *affaires de coeur* for which the only proviso was that there should be no scandal and no discreet tea parties while the husband of his hostess sat drinking at his Club until it was time for him to go home for dinner.

There would be no scented *billets-doux*, no conveniently placed adjacent bedrooms in country house parties and certainly he would not invite to his own home the type of men like himself, who would undoubtedly want to make love to anyone as beautiful as Nelda.

'I love her! She is *mine*!' he admitted finally, fiercely and determinedly.

He went to his bedroom to lie awake with the wheels of the train rumbling under him and repeating over and over again.

"I love her! *I love her*!"

*

In the morning when he was dressed Lord Harleston went into the drawing room to find that he was to breakfast alone.

"I looked in at the young lady, my Lord," the servant told him, "but she was sleepin' so peaceful I left her."

"Quite right," Lord Harleston approved.

He knew that if Nelda could sleep it would be the best thing possible for her.

Although she had been so brave, although she had forced herself when they reached the Ranch to try to behave normally, the unhappiness she felt at losing her father and mother and the ordeals that she had had to face afterwards would have taken their toll of anyone let alone a young girl.

"Sleep is the best healer," he remembered his mother saying when he was a small boy.

He thought that Nelda needed healing and sleep would be more effective than any words of sympathy or a doctor's medicine.

She did not wake until late in the afternoon.

When she joined Lord Harleston, she looked, with her flushed cheeks and eyes still a little hazy, so lovely that it was with the greatest difficulty that he did not put his arms around her and tell her so.

"I-I am sorry," she murmured.

"There is nothing to be sorry for," he smiled.

"I have never slept so long before in my whole life. I seemed to be floating on a cloud and now I feel as if centuries of time have gone by and I have missed them."

"You have missed nothing, except for miles and miles of very empty country."

She gave a little laugh and sat down opposite him to gaze out of the window.

"When I came this way before," she said, "I kept thinking that America is very very big."

"And you will find England very very small," Lord Harleston replied.

He saw by the little flutter of her eyelashes that the idea of going to England intimidated her and he added hurriedly,

"But we will not be going there for a long time yet, so we will be able to appreciate the largeness of America together."

He knew by the way her expression changed that she had not missed how he had used the word '*we*'.

There was a little pause and then she asked,

"Could we not – be alone – you and I?"

"That is what I would like," Lord Harleston said, "but I understand that Waldo has different ideas."

"I-I don't – wish to – see him."

The words seemed to slip through her lips as if she could not prevent saying them.

"Why do you say that?" Lord Harleston asked quietly.

Nelda looked down at her hands, which, clasped together, were on the table in front of her.

She was choosing her words with care before she responded,

"He – he said – things to me I did not – like."

"What sort of things? "

"He said he – loved me and I must – marry him."

Then, with a frantic note in her voice, Nelda went on,

"I don't have to marry him, do I? You will not – make me?"

"Let me make this clear," Lord Harleston replied, "and this is a promise, Nelda. I will never make you marry anyone you don't wish to marry."

"You really – promise?"

"I never break my word and I have no wish for you to marry Waldo Altman or any other man at the moment."

He nearly added, 'except for myself', but he knew that it was much too soon to say anything of the sort and he would only scare her.

She looked up at him and her eyes shone as if there was a light in them.

"Now I am happy!" she exclaimed. "I have been frightened – very frightened that you would want me to marry Waldo since that would be a – convenient way of getting rid of me."

Because this thought had actually passed through Lord Harleston's mind at one time, he felt ashamed.

"Forget him!" he exclaimed. "You need not see him again if you don't want to. But, Nelda, you must be aware that you are very beautiful and there will always be men who will tell you so."

"I don't want to – listen to – them."

"But one day you will fall in love," Lord Harleston insisted.

She smiled at him.

"It would be like Papa and Mama and it would be – different."

"But of course," Lord Harleston agreed, "and I think the true love that your father and mother had for each other is what we all seek in our lives."

"You understand! You really understand!" Nelda cried. "Oh, I am so glad."

"Of course I understand," Lord Harleston said in his deep voice, "because that is what I am looking for myself."

His eyes were on Nelda's face as he spoke, hoping for some response.

But she merely said,

"Oh, I do hope you find it, but you may have to seek it for a very long time. Papa said he thought for years that he would never really fall in love until he met Mama."

"In the past I have had all the wrong ideas about your father and mother," Lord Harleston admitted. "Now you tell me how happy they were together and how hard your father worked, even though it was at cards, to make money for you and your mother and I am beginning to understand."

He paused, saw that Nelda was listening to him and went on,

"The love they had for each other was worth being exiled from England, from their relations, from their friends and from everything that mattered to your father when he was a young man."

Nelda smiled and Lord Harleston thought that the curve of her lips was the most enchanting thing he had ever seen.

"I wish Papa could have heard you say that. He was often, I think, homesick for England and especially for the house where you live. He said it was the centre of the family and, as long as it was standing the Harles would always feel that there was one place where they belonged, and where, when the time came, they would like to – die."

She looked at Lord Harleston sadly as she emphasised,

"Papa had a great sympathy – for the Indians. He felt that they had been badly treated and I don't think it ever crossed his mind that they would – kill him."

"When we go home," Lord Harleston said gently, "I am going to suggest that you and I put up a memorial stone for your father and mother in the Church at Harleston Park, where so many of our relatives have been both baptised and buried."

"That would be wonderful!" Nelda exclaimed. "Thank you, thank you for thinking of anything so kind. I know it will please Papa and Mama."

She spoke almost as if they would know about it and Lord Harleston realised that she thought of them as being still alive and, although she could not see them, near to her and still loving her.

He had never had such thoughts about a woman before and it struck him to his surprise that, while he had so much to teach Nelda, perhaps there were things she could teach him.

They talked of many things while tea was brought to them and went on talking until dinnertime.

Then, as if she could not help it, Nelda burst out impulsively,

"It's so marvellous to be with you. It's like being with Papa and yet different in that you are almost like somebody from another planet and I have so much to learn from you."

Lord Harleston felt a thrill of delight run through him at her words.

"If it is marvellous for you to learn from me, it is exciting for me to teach you. I have never had a pupil before and certainly not such an attentive one."

"Perhaps you will grow bored with all the questions I shall ask you."

Lord Harleston smiled.

"I only hope that I will not prove to be too ignorant to have the right replies to them."

She laughed as if that was impossible and said,

"It is like having an encyclopaedia all to myself. I want to go on reading, reading and turning the pages and finding new subjects on every one."

With difficulty Lord Harleston prevented himself from telling her that there was really only one subject he wanted to talk about and that was himself and what she felt about him.

Instead he suggested,

"Go to bed, Nelda, and sleep as well as you did last night. We don't arrive in New York until noon."

She hesitated and enthused,

"It's so fantastic being with you! I am half-afraid if I go to bed I shall find in the morning that it has all been a dream and you are not – here."

"I promise you I will be here," Lord Harleston answered positively.

He spoke softly and insistently and, as Nelda glanced at him, he thought, if he managed to hold her eyes for a moment, there would be some response to the yearning in his own.

But she rose to her feet saying,

"Goodnight and thank you, my Lord. Thank you for being so kind to me."

She put out her hand towards him.

Then, as he rose to his feet to take it in his own, the train gave a sudden jerk, she stumbled and he put out his arms to prevent her from falling.

Just for a moment he held her close against him and, as she laughed up at him, it was with the greatest difficulty that he did not kiss her.

"I am sorry for being so clumsy," she said. "Goodnight."

"Goodnight," Lord Harleston replied and reluctantly took his arms from her.

She walked towards her bedroom, and only when she was out of sight did he sit down and wonder how long it would be before he could tell her exactly what was in his mind, in his heart and in his soul.

*

"I have never owned so many gowns before!" Nelda cried. "They are just like the gowns Mama and I used to dream we would buy one day if ever Papa made enough money."

She was looking at the clothes that had been delivered to their apartment after they had spent the previous day shopping in New York.

They had spent what seemed to Nelda to be an astronomical amount of money, but Lord Harleston had insisted that she bought every gown that he admired her in.

They had also ordered a great number of others to be made from materials they had chosen in the styles that were, they were assured, new from Paris.

Lord Harleston had at many times chosen gowns for the beauties who were content for him to pay for them and there had been a very pretty little dancer from the Ballet who, exquisite in every other way, had appalling taste when it came to clothes.

He therefore fancied himself as an expert and thought that he must have known when he had first seen her in her torn and dusty dress lying on the bed in Jennie Rogers's house that she would look very different when elegantly gowned.

When he had been angry at having to rescue her from being made into 'a boarder', he was concerned with her appearance as one of the family and not as a beautiful woman.

Now, as every gown Nelda put on seemed more becoming and a better frame for her beauty than the last, Lord Harleston found it enthralling to see her look even lovelier than she had ever looked before.

When she was wearing a silk gown as blue as the sky, he thought that only an artist like Fragonard could paint her portrait and express not only her beauty and grace but something else that he had never found in any other woman.

The more he was with Nelda, the more he realised that she had a spiritual aura that came not from her perfect features and not from the colour of her hair, but from some inner light within her.

It shone through her and made him more and more aware every day that she had an exceptional personality besides being utterly and completely desirable as a woman.

He found himself enchanted by her brain, which was quick, retentive and amazingly original.

As he had complained to Robert, the women he made love to seldom said anything that he did not expect them to say and he had added cynically the epithet that '*all cats in the dark are grey*'.

But Nelda was quite different.

He found that he could never anticipate in advance what would be her attitude on any particular subject and he could not remember her saying anything banal or making a remark that would have been better left unsaid.

He found his love for her increasing day-by-day and hour-by-hour and sometimes it was an agony to pretend an indifference that he did not feel and to conceal the emotions that seemed to consume him.

For the first time in his life he was thinking of somebody else rather than of himself. He knew that it was because he was the only person now in her life, one unwary or hasty word could destroy her trust and sense of security and she would be alone and perhaps desperately unhappy.

Because he loved her so deeply, this was a risk he could not take.

He therefore schooled himself to talk to Nelda naturally and without sounding too personal and to ensure that every moment they were together she grew to rely on him more and more and he prayed to love him as he loved her.

Letters and flowers arrived from Waldo every day.

If he asked if he could see Nelda, she did not say so and Lord Harleston deliberately did not ask enquire into what she read in his letters.

They went to the theatre where she sat entranced like a child at its first pantomime, to the Ballet and to the New Metropolitan Opera House where they had a box to themselves, which she found delightful.

As they were staying in the apartment of the Prairie Cattle Company, the Press were not aware that Lord Harleston had returned to New York, as they would have done had he been staying in a hotel or with a prestigious family.

He was careful not to appear in restaurants or places where he was likely to meet somebody he knew or just be recognised.

To be with Nelda was a joy in itself and at the same time an agony because he loved her so much that he found it hard to sleep when she was only the width of the passage away from him.

'How can I go on like this?' he asked himself dozens of times.

Yet he was still too nervous to take the plunge and ask Nelda what she felt about him.

He knew now as her eyes lit up when she came into the room where he was sitting after dinner, and she left him reluctantly because she wished to go on talking to him.

He had the uncomfortable feeling that she still thought of him as an elderly Guardian who had taken the place of her father.

'What can I do? How can I make her aware of me as a man?' he asked the sky and then he laughed mockingly at himself.

In the past there had never been a woman who he had been alone with for a few minutes without her making it obvious that she thought him an attractive man and a very desirable one at that.

But, when Nelda slipped her hand into his when they were walking along the corridor, he knew that it was the touch of a confiding child.

"I love her! *I love her*!" Lord Harleston repeated over and over again.

When she came into the room to show him a new evening gown before they went out to dinner, he would feel the blood throbbing in his temples and he felt that one day his will would snap and he would take her in his arms and kiss her as his lips burned to do.

"Goodnight, it has been a wonderful, wonderful evening, just like – all the rest we have spent together," Nelda would say.

"I have enjoyed it too," Lord Harleston would answer.

"You are quite sure that you have not been bored?"

"Not for a moment."

"I am very very glad. I am frightened of boring you because I am so ignorant and sometimes you must find me very – foolish."

"I have never found you foolish."

"And I pray you never – will. Thank you again – and goodnight, my Lord."

"Goodnight, Nelda."

She would leave him, but he wanted to hold on to her to keep her with him.

She would give him an entrancing little smile as she reached the door. Yet he knew that there was not the look in her eyes that he so wanted to see.

Then she had gone and he would think despairingly that he would have another wakeful night yearning for her.

They had been nearly a week in New York when one very hot day they were sitting in the lounge of their apartment talking and a servant opened the door to announce,

"Mr. Waldo Altman Junior, my Lord!"

Lord Harleston, who was lying back in his chair, then sat up rapidly and Nelda gave a little exclamation.

Waldo, holding a huge bunch of orchids, came across the room.

"I had to come and see you," he said to Nelda, "as you don't answer my letters."

Nelda rose slowly to her feet and, as Waldo held out the orchids, she took them from him automatically and then put them down on a side table.

"How can you be so cruel, Nelda, when I told you how much I wanted to see you?" he asked. "I've been waiting every day for a reply."

As Nelda obviously found it difficult to find words to answer him with, Lord Harleston said,

"We have been very busy, Waldo."

"How are you, my Lord?" Waldo asked as if he suddenly realised that he was in the room.

"I thought perhaps you would come to New York," Lord Harleston remarked.

"I have written to Nelda every day to tell her so," Waldo said with a reproachful look at her.

"As I have just said, we have been very busy," Lord Harleston repeated, "and we are extremely grateful to your father for allowing us to stay here. It has been most convenient as well as comfortable."

He spoke meaningfully, thinking it only right that Nelda should be aware that she was, one might almost say, a guest of Mr. Altman.

"I'm glad you are comfortable here," Waldo replied.

He was not looking at Lord Harleston but at Nelda.

"I have to see you," he said urgently as if they were alone. "I have to talk to you."

Nelda gave a little cry.

"No! There is – nothing to say – nothing at all!"

She looked appealingly at Lord Harleston as she spoke and he interposed,

"I think perhaps you should have a word alone with Waldo. After all he has come all this way to see you."

"I have – nothing to say to him – nothing!" Nelda asserted. "Please – please – send him away – and I don't want any more – letters from him."

She ran as she spoke towards Lord Harleston to hold onto his arm with both hands.

"Please – send him – away," she pleaded.

As if he felt somewhat embarrassed, Lord Harleston turned to say,

"I am sorry, Waldo, but as I have told you before, it is up to Nelda."

As he spoke, he had the feeling that Waldo was not listening.

Instead he was looking at Nelda, his eyes taking in the expression on her face as she appealed to Lord Harleston for help and the way she was holding onto his arm with both hands.

Waldo looked at her for a long moment and then he said,

"So that's how it is! I guess it's what I might have expected. All right, go ahead and marry him! But I warn you, his reputation's worse than your father's and he'll make you unhappy. You'll be a hell of a lot worse off with him than you would be with me!"

As he finished speaking, his voice had risen to a shout.

Then he turned on his heel, stalked out of the room and slammed the door behind him.

For a moment Nelda stood as if turned to stone.

Then, as if the full impact of what Waldo had said swept over her, she made a convulsive little sound and turned to hide her head against Lord Harleston's shoulder.

His arms went round her and he held her against him.

She was crying and in a voice he could hardly hear she stammered hesitantly,

"I-I am sorry – I did not – want you to – know – !"

His arms tightened and he asked in a tone that he could hardly recognise as his own,

"Are you saying, Nelda, that you love me?"

He was aware that she took a deep breath before she replied,

"I-I cannot – help it – please don't – send me away!"

There was a frantic note in her voice as she lifted her face to look up at him pleadingly and her eyes wet with tears were held by Lord Harleston's so that it was impossible to look away.

"*You love me!*" he said slowly as if he could hardly believe that it was the truth. "Oh, my darling, you have crucified me because I thought I would never be able to tell you how much I love *you!*"

She stared at him.

Then the light that came into her face was dazzling.

"You – you – *love me*?" she questioned beneath her breath.

"I adore and worship you!" Lord Harleston answered. "I have loved you for so long I feel as if it has been a century of time, but I did not dare to ask what you felt about me."

"I love you – so much that I have been – terrified you would – send me to England and I have been – praying and – praying that I could – stay with you."

"Your prayers have been heard," Lord Harleston said. "You will stay with me, my darling, for the rest of our lives and now I can teach you about love, which is something I have been yearning to do."

As he spoke, he drew her closer still and his lips found hers.

He kissed her very gently because he was afraid of frightening her, then, as he felt almost as if she melted into him, his lips became more demanding, more insistent and even more possessive.

As he felt the softness of her lips, he felt an ecstasy that he had never known before in the whole of his life flood through him and knew as it did so that she was feeling the same.

It was so wonderful, so rapturous and so different from the fiery desire that a kiss had meant to him in the past that for a moment he could hardly believe that what he was feeling was true and he was not dreaming.

Then, as he felt Nelda's mouth quiver and he knew her body was trembling, not from fear but with the rapture of his kisses, he became more passionate and demanding.

He knew then that this was what he had longed for, searched for and thought he would never find.

To Nelda it was as if the Heavens opened and Lord Harleston swept her into the celestial light and she was blinded by the glory of it.

She knew that this was the love that her father and mother had known and which she swore long ago in her dreams that she would seek and, if she did not find it, then she would never love anybody or let any man touch her.

Waldo Altman had been so certain that she would do what he wanted and she knew that, unless Lord Harleston protected her, she would have nowhere to hide from him.

At first she had felt that he was a tower of strength, someone who had taken her father's place, until the more she was with him the more she felt as if he was not only there to look after her but she had become a part of him.

When she went to bed at night, she dreamt of him and, when she woke in the morning, her first thought was that she would see him and be with him.

Still for a long time she had not understood until her instinct had told her that as far as she was concerned he was the only man in the world and, if she could not be with him, she would rather die.

Even then she did not realise completely that she loved him as a man and it was rather that he was larger than life and an integral part of her prayers, her thoughts and her dreams.

It was only when Waldo wanted to marry her that she knew that there was only one man she wanted to marry, although she was sure that he would never want to marry her.

And that was Lord Harleston.

'How could he – want me when he thinks I am just a – child and a very tiresome – encumbrance?' she often asked herself despairingly.

She was terrified that he might guess her feelings for him and it would not only disgust him but persuade him to send her to England even sooner than he intended.

Because her mother had always taught her to be controlled and not to show her feelings and her father had said that nothing annoyed him more than a woman who cried and whined to get her own way, Nelda was able to hide her love.

But sometimes she felt Lord Harleston must guess that she wanted to be near him, wanted to touch him and to be quite certain that he was really there.

'I love him! *I love him!*' she had said to herself on the train when they had talked together.

It was an agony for her to leave him at night and go to her own room knowing that she wanted to stay with him and to lie beside him as they had in the farmhouse.

'Why did I not know then that I loved him?' she asked herself.

She knew, however, that, if her mind had not accepted that it was love, her instinct had done so when she had slipped her hand into his and felt safe and at peace because he was beside her.

Now at the touch of his lips she knew what she had thought was true, she belonged to him and was a part of him that was indivisible.

Only when they touched the very zenith of ecstasy and it seemed that only human frailty prevented it from being prolonged for ever, did Lord Harleston raise his head and they came back to earth.

"I love you!" he sighed in his deep voice. "How could I have known that you would make me feel like this?"

"Like – what?" Nelda asked, her eyes shining, her lips parted with the feelings of wonder that he had aroused in her.

"I am no longer a man, my darling," he said. "Because you love me I am a God! Just now we touched Heaven together and our lives will never be the same again."

Nelda gave a cry of happiness.

"I feel it too! We feel the same way, think the same and now you love me I want to go down on my knees and thank God as this is what I have prayed and prayed for."

"I have prayed as well," Lord Harleston said. "Oh, my precious, my adorable one, how can I have been so fortunate and so incredibly lucky as to have found you?"

"If you are lucky – I am lucky too."

She hesitated for a moment before she added wistfully,

"You – did say you – wanted to – marry me?"

"I am going to marry you immediately," Lord Harleston answered. "You will be my wife, my precious one, and nothing and nobody shall ever frighten or upset you again."

"I could never be – frightened with – you and I want to go on saying – over and over again – I love you!"

It was, however, impossible to do so because Lord Harleston kissed her again, holding her lips captive once more until they both felt as if they were floating above the world and were no longer human.

He kissed her until they could no longer stand and sank down onto the sofa with their arms entwined and Nelda's head on his shoulder.

He kissed her forehead, her eyes, her little straight nose and lastly her mouth.

"What I want to do now," he said when he could speak, "is to find out how we can be married and how quickly I can make you my wife."

"I want to be your – wife today!"

"That is what I want too, but it may take a little longer, my lovely one."

She rose to her feet to go and stand at the window.

They were many floors up and they looked out at the high buildings, the roofs and trees of New York.

"Because you love me, this is Paradise," Lord Harleston said, "but I really want to take you home, my darling, home to England where we both belong."

"It does not matter – where I am – so long as I am with you," Nelda sighed, "and I feel that even your – relatives will not be – unkind about Papa – if you are with me."

"You may be certain of that," he said, "and not '*my* relatives', my darling but '*our* relatives'."

"I like being a Harle, it makes me closer to you," Nelda murmured simply.

He kissed her because she was just so adorable and then, as the door opened, they moved reluctantly apart.

It was a servant bringing in a cable.

As Lord Harleston took it from him, he felt that he knew already what it contained, but told himself that he was being over-optimistic.

He opened it and for a moment the words seemed to dance in front of his eyes.

Then he forced himself to read it carefully so that there would be no mistake.

He read,

"Dolly announcing her engagement tomorrow to Elmsdale.
Come home. Missing you.
Robert."

Lord Harleston knew that the Earl of Elmsdale was a very wealthy Peer who had been in love with Dolly for some time.

He gave a deep sigh as if a burden had fallen from his shoulders.

"What – is it? What has – happened?" Nelda asked him.

"I have just turned up another ace," he replied, "and, because it is so amazingly lucky, my precious, I think perhaps your father's mantle has fallen on me and, if that is true, I am very grateful."

She looked puzzled and he explained,

"This is a cable to say that we can go home. One day I will tell you all about it, but not now."

He smiled as he went on,

"If we were sensible we would wait and be married with all our relatives there to see us, but instead I am going to marry you tomorrow, here in New York, so that we can travel home as man and wife."

As he spoke, he knew, although perhaps it was not so romantic, that it was a prudent thing to do so that there would be no question of Nelda being compromised if she was alone with him.

No one in England would ever be aware that they had spent these days together and the news of what had happened in Denver was not likely to percolate to Buckinghamshire or London.

"I would – rather be married here – so that I can be – alone with you." Nelda said.

"That is what I want too," Lord Harleston replied, "and, darling, does it really matter where we are? We have already been in some strange places together and I think it has taught us that the only thing of any consequence in our lives is our love for each other."

Nelda put her arms around his neck to draw his head down to hers.

"I am so – happy, so wildly wonderfully – happy that I can hardly believe I could be – happier when we are – married."

"I will make you happy," Lord Harleston promised. "I will teach you about love, my adorable beautiful wife and make you aware that the love I have for you fills my whole world until there is no room for anything else."

She gave a little cry of delight.

And then she said,

"We have – found each other and now all I want to do is to – love you from now until – Eternity. We are lucky in love."

"And the love I have for you," Lord Harleston added, "will protect and keep you safe and, my darling, prevent you from ever being frightened by anything as long as we are together."

"I – love you!" Nelda whispered.

Then his lips were on hers and she could no longer speak, but only feel, as he was, that they were flying into the Light of God and the world was left behind them.

OTHER BOOKS IN THIS SERIES

The Barbara Cartland Eternal Collection is the unique opportunity to collect all five hundred of the timeless beautiful romantic novels written by the world's most celebrated and enduring romantic author.

Named the Eternal Collection because Barbara's inspiring stories of pure love, just the same as love itself, the books will be published on the internet at the rate of four titles per month until all five hundred are available.

The Eternal Collection, classic pure romance available worldwide for all time.